Nothing is as it seems...

mrs.

deveraux

OTHER BOOKS BY ALINA

Deceptive Men
Through the Eyes of a Mother

mrs. deveraux

The Art of Power, Seduction, & Murder

alina

E.L. Pilton Publishing Co.
Visit us at: www.alinabooks.com

ALINA BOOKS are published by

EL Pilton Publishing Co., Plano, Texas 75025

www.alinabooks.com

This book is a work of **fiction**. Names, characters, businesses, organizations, places, and incidents are either products of the author's imagination or used *fictitiously*. All characters are fictional, and any similarity to people living or dead, events or locales is purely coincidental.

Library of Congress Cataloging-in-Publication Data

Alina, —
    Mrs. Deveraux / Alina.

    ISBN 978-0-9887933-1-6 (Paperback)
    ISBN 978-0-9887933-2-3 (eBook)

    1. Michigan— Fiction. 2. Detroit— Fiction. 3. Bloomfield Hills (homicide/murders, etc)— Fiction. 4. Oakland County— Fiction. 5. Detroit Newspaper/Free Press— Fiction. 6. Wayne County— Fiction. Mrs. Julie Ann Deveraux— *Fictitious Character*. I. Title

Printed in the United States of America
Cover Design by Angel A. Allen

To Burger, who inspired me to keep moving!

in•trigue **A**v. /in'trēg/ (**intriguing, intrigued**) — **1** [trans.] arouse the curiosity or interest of; fascinate. **2** [intrans.] make secret plans to do something illicit or detrimental to someone. **A**n. /'in, trēg/ **1** the secret planning of something illicit or detrimental…a secret love affair. **2** a mysterious or fascinating quality (**in•tri•guing•ly**) **adv**.— *Mrs. Deveraux is intriguingly interesting. Her monstrous intrigue frightens your senses.*

—*The Oxford American Dictionary*

Chapter 1

A Killing of a Thousand Words

AFTER LYING IN WAIT FOR MORE THAN FOUR hours, the predator finally made his move. The killer unsuccessfully tried to keep quiet to startle his prey. His efforts were challenged by the earsplitting floorboards as he forcefully tried to silence them with every step. He knew exactly where he wanted to go and what he needed to do. He knew this was the only way he could destroy his past.

It was fifteen minutes after three. His victims would be sound asleep this time of morning.

alina

Overexerted from the intensity of the moments, the killer sighed heavily once he made his way up the lengthy spiral staircase, passed the guest quarters, and to the end of a narrow hallway that led to his victim's bedroom. He had walked these floors before but never in the dark. He struggled from side to side in the deep darkness, hands slightly tapping the walls to guide his direction. Just a few more steps, he thought to himself.

At last, he reached a half-closed door in the southwest end of the mansion, the master suite. He carefully opened the door with the tip of his pistol, not anticipating shooting his prey; but then again, he hadn't decided on a plan.

The door moved smoothly without a sound. An unimportant grin drifted across his face. He walked through the bedroom door with gentle steps. After several feet, his steps came to a halt and his body jerked in panic. "They should be asleep," he quietly mumbled to himself, not realizing that the man before him had simply rolled over in a routine turn. Startled by the sudden movement from the gentlemen lying in bed next to his wife; the killer swiftly wrapped his body around the back of the bedroom door. He stood between the wall and the door— heart pounding through his chest, breath moving in a steady but heavy flow. He tucked the pistol under his left armpit and massaged his moistened left hand with his right. He glanced down at his hands and with a beam of light that gleamed through the bedroom window from an undrawn portion of the curtains; he could see his hands trembling and palms glossy. He felt a sudden gust of heat invade his face; and he noticed moist drippings falling onto his hands. He was sweating profusely. He shook his head, trying to knock out the fear, but nothing worked.

"Pull yourself together you blundering idiot," he mumbled to himself. With the pounding of his heart increasing, his eyes flickered in panic. "Just do it," he whispered.

He glanced at the handcrafted fireplace to the left of him. He took an immense breath and pulled away from the door; moved quickly across the room and yanked out a blow poke. With the pistol in one hand and the blow poke in the other, he contemplated on his next move. He had not really planned this perfectly, if he seriously considered a plan at all. He just knew this man had to die. His wife had to go too.

Equally exasperated and nauseated, he made it to the bed where the couple lay sleeping. In a single sweep, he glanced over the couple and the room with restricted view. He pondered if he could go through with this but it was too late to turn back now. He had made it this far. He had already selected the burial site and the graves were dug. It was the perfect area. An old abandoned building on Detroit's Westside. He had dug an eight-foot grave, making sure the grave was deep enough for *all* the bodies.

Now, standing beside the bed as the couple lay sleeping, he wondered if it was all worth it. Would he be able to get away with this— of course he would.

Just in that instant the old man woke up. "Who's there?" he said in a groggy tone, trying to focus in the nearly dark room. The old man tried to clear his vision; squinting his eyes while blinking hurriedly. He raised his torso and aggressively cleared his throat as if he was about to take an important phone call.

Stunned by the man's words and sudden movement, the killer held his pistol in the air pointing it toward the old man's head. The old man stretched out his hand and turned on the light.

"I say, who goes there…" Before he could finish his statement, he paused, recognizing the man standing before him. "What the hell are you doing here?" he said very angrily.

"*Shut-up*. You don't get to do the talking anymore," he said nervously.

"You're as stupid as I knew you to be. You're no grand…"

He tuned out the old man's voice, tossed the pistol on the foot of the bed and swung the blow poke with all the strength he had. The first swing nearly took the old man's head off. He heard a crack and thought he had broken his neck with the first swing. By this time, the old man's wife had awakened, still deeply under like a spell;

and as she slightly lifted her body, the killer swung the blow poke again.

The first blow to the wife's head knocked her back to the bed but she was still moving. He improvised. He ran back to the fireplace and grabbed an antique candle stick holder that he could grip a little better. He shuffled around the room in an impromptu panic. He hit the wife over the head again and again and again. The superfluous blows to the wife's head were gruesome but somewhat hesitant. Blood fanned across the ceiling and cascaded transversely down the headboard of the bed.

Then he ran to the other side of the bed, hit the old man again across the head with the candle stick holder. Presuming that the first blow to the head had killed him, the killer wanted to be sure that the old man was dead. He dragged the old man's body from the bed onto the floor and laid him spread eagle across the carpet. He placed his body on top of the old man's stomach, as if he thought the old man was going to get away. He stared at the man's body for a moment, and then he started his crazed thrust. He struck the old man over thirty times beyond recognition before he would end his madness. It was pure hatred driving the arm that turned this night into a murder massacre.

Chapter 2

Mrs. Deveraux's Allies

IG BURLY MAN, REFINED DARK BROWN HAIR WITH gray cascading along the edges of his hairline, serious brow, and a seasoned cop swag; Sergeant Willowbee wasn't easily intimidated. But the monstrous wind that often blew his way left a sense of powerlessness that entranced you. Mrs. Deveraux had that effect on people – *and it was lethal*.

"I can't keep covering up for you Mrs. Deveraux," Sergeant Willowbee stated as cautiously as he could, fearing an unfavorable response that could have him seeking a new profession.

Julie Ann Deveraux was not use to hearing the word *no*; merely understanding the word's meaning was a challenge for her. She glanced at Sgt. Willowbee, still standing next to the guest chair in Sgt. Willowbee's office and with little emotion she responded, "Oh, Bill, we've went over this travesty before. You know that my husband is in a very uncompromising position here. It would be detrimental to our reputation if it gets out into the media that we could be connected to these horrendous crimes. That is why I am demanding your help."

"But they are crawling up my ass now and pretty soon, they are going to blame me for withholding evidence or obstruction of justice. And if they play *real* dirty, they could very well toss in conspiracy to commit murder." Hands unnoticeably shaking, speech slightly slurred, and Sgt. Willowbee's eyes gleamed with a hint of flustered fear and anxiety. His anxiety was deeply inscribed into the core of his gut and he felt nauseated.

He proclaimed he was done covering Mrs. Deveraux's destructive trail. Or so he thought. It did seem sort of odd that there was a small connection between Mr. and Mrs. Deveraux and the murdered victims. But Sgt. Willowbee didn't want to mull over this too long because he didn't have that luxury. He was fighting to keep his own sanity (and his job) in this complex saga. He certainly didn't have the means or the energy to tangle with one of the richest, most powerful, and prominent woman in the state, he thought.

"Don't worry about that right now," she said in a resounding tone and placed her bottom in one of the guest chairs and then continued, "I said I would take care of you, didn't I? Now, I just need you to retrieve the files from the drawer."

"*Files*." He declared excitedly. "You didn't say anything about any files."

"They're my Quitclaim Deed papers. I simply forgot to get them from Mr. Holmes during our luncheon yesterday, that's all. I am this close to finalizing this project and claiming my building and land." She looked at Sgt. Willowbee with a fierce expression. Mrs. Deveraux had come too far and she was not going to give up now. "I need those papers, Mr. Willowbee," she stated in a steady firm, heart piercing voice. Her provocative tone cut right through you and her words pained you like fingers plunging into a wound.

"And how do you suppose I get these files? Do you expect me to walk out of a crime scene with files under my arm?" he annoyed tone was clear and precise.

"You are a very clever man, Mr. Willowbee; I'm sure you will figure it out," she answered with a smug smile as she reached across the desk and delicately tapped Sgt. Willowbee on the left cheek. Her eloquent touch felt like silk and her alluring stare restricted you. Even though her painstaking guttural voice broke you from her spell, you were still left with a lasting impression that overwhelmed your psyche.

It seemed to be more and more difficult for Sgt. Willowbee to break from Mrs. Deveraux's spell. He couldn't understand why such desire aroused for her. He was a man of the law and such desires were forbidden, but there was something about Mrs. Deveraux that made you forget who you are and why you are here.

"That's the problem, Mrs. Deveraux; I can't get away with that. We have to tag and bag any and everything that leaves the crime scene."

Mrs. Deveraux stood up from the cheaply made leather chair and walked toward the door; glancing back at Sgt. Willowbee with those glowing mesmerizing brown eyes and said sharply, "Just think of it as if your life depended on it."

With a wink of an eye and a candid smile, she exited Sgt. Willowbee's office at the Bloomfield Hills Police Department.

Chapter 3

For the Art of it All

I T WAS A BLOODY MESS, ONE OF THE HOMICIDE detectives depicted the aftermath of the crime scene at the Holmes Estate. Sgt. Willowbee entered the door with extreme caution, patrolling his surroundings and feeling the intense irregular beat of his heart while scanning the scene for the lead detective. "They are going to wonder why I am here," he thought to himself. "I haven't thought of what I would say if I am confronted. This is pathetic," he whispered to himself. "How did I get so deep into this mess?" His thoughts lingered for what seemed like forever before his mind registered a muffled voice in the distance.

"Sgt. Willowbee, are you okay?" A seasoned detective shouted for the third time, trying to get Sgt. Willowbee's attention.

Sgt. Willowbee's body jerked from the trance and quickly answered, "Yes. Yeah, I'm okay. What a mess," he added to smooth over the awkwardness of that stunned moment.

"Yeah, this makes the fourth victim, well, eighth when you count their wives too," Detective Jarrod stated with exhaustion releasing a hefty sigh.

"Any possible leads here besides the *zero leads* we have back at the station?"

"Not a one," Det. Jarrod said in dismay.

"The Feds are crawling up our ass now and we don't have a single clue to who the perpetrator might be. How in the hell did the Feds get involved in this anyway?" Sgt. Willowbee asked with mild frustration.

Det. Jarrod took out his little black notepad and flipped through the pages from several nights before and replied, "Looks like our third family, The Palowski's. Mr. Palowski was the brother of this hard ass FBI agent and somehow he convinced the bureau that there was a connection somewhere and that their presence was needed in this investigation."

"A connection to what?" Sgt. Willowbee asked.

"I don't know. But his boys have been sniffing around since last week. It may be a connection but I seriously doubt it. He's trying to find the person that killed his brother, plain and simple."

"Just what we need," Sgt. Willowbee said while taking an exhaustive breath.

A commotion outside quickly interrupted their recap and shifted their attention to the front entrance of the estate. As Det. Jarrod and Sgt. Willowbee glanced out the window, they could see the rookies that were placed at the front gate to fan off unwanted guess trying to hold back a man that was trying to enter the premises.

"It doesn't look like they are doing a good job holding him back," Det. Jarrod stated. "Let me send Detective Willington and Bagger to assist those darn rookies." Det. Jarrod sighed in much frustration and whispered, "Damn rookies…not today."

Sgt. Willowbee unknowingly followed Det. Jarrod to the study of the Holmes Estate where the murder took place. After all, it was routine. Det. Jarrod was too consumed with trying to keep control of his crime scene, the estate, and anything that may be a potential lead, to even contemplate on why Sgt. Willowbee was at his crime scene.

Sgt. Willowbee realized that he was now where he needed to be if he was going to walk out with those files. He strongly considered turning around and explaining to Mrs. Deveraux that he wasn't able to retrieve the files. He rejected the idea from his head and immediately knew it was a toxic thought.

He had been on the police force for over thirty years and he knew that this was a bad idea. He had seen cops go downhill for helping the wealthy and powerful. He had seen it often where a detective believed the story of a person presumably innocent and it turned out to be a deplorable mistake. He had seen many cops' careers go down the sewer because they were coerced into being a part of a scandal.

Sgt. Willowbee wasn't ready for his brush with death. He wasn't ready to be condemned for someone else's evildoing but here he was, in the home of a murdered victim, stealing files for a powerful woman that should be considered a prime suspect.

"How did I get so deep into this mess...hell, I don't even know what mess I'm in," he infuriatingly whispered to himself. He tried to convince himself that these were extenuating circumstances and that he really had no choice. He tried to convince himself that he was just a peon in this complex circle of the powerful and the wealthy, and he was only doing as he was told. No matter how he swung the excuses, he simply couldn't bring himself to believe he didn't have a choice—*no matter how convincing it sounded.*

He browsed across the room before soaking in the scene. He forcefully tried to swallow a hard lump that lingered in his throat as he peeked at Mr. Holmes' body (or body parts) that lay orderly across the floor. Their bodies were not covered up at this point because the CSI's were still analyzing the scene; seemingly irritated by the countless number of police and detectives that trampled the crime scene.

That's why they wore fiber-free overalls and gloves, to avoid contaminating the crime scene. They photographed; performed a strip search method; marked and packaged potential evidence (although the murder weapon was never left at the scene and the killer always used a different gun, but the same caliber); and jotted down notes.

Most of the photos of the crime scene and *so-called* evidence bared nothing more but that the authorities had a sophisticated serial killer on their hands. The police had no idea where to search for the killer or what his next move would be or who his next target was. The killer had always taken his time with his victims; stalking them, lying in wait, knowing just when to strike. He would always cut the husband's limbs off, neatly placing them alongside each other.

From the very first killing – *Ronald and Debra Smits* – his meticulous nature suggested a professional. It was likely he had killed before but those killings were never connected to any of these new heinous crimes, most of the detectives thought. No, this was overkill and motivated by something other than the thrill, Det. Jarrod once stated. He's looking for something or trying to stop something from happening, he continued to proclaim. Det. Jarrod knew that he was right; he just needed to prove it.

While the CSI's were in the adjacent room photographing Mrs. Holmes, Sgt. Willowbee focused on his mission. He managed a swallow and narrowed his eyes toward the huge executive desk several feet in front of him. He had known from the many visits to Jim Holmes estate that he was a very orderly gentleman. Holmes would have notepads, papers, pens and pencils, business cards, and desk accessories all angled systematically throughout the space of the desk and each in its place. Not today. The desk was in shambles. Sgt. Willowbee hadn't noticed an odd painting that protruded from underneath a handful of scattered papers. He passed over the painting and scanned across the top layer of documents. It appeared to have been a tussle of some kind, which was not typical of the other three murdered victims. It seemed to have been two separate instances that took place minutes apart from the other, Sgt. Willowbee mentally noted.

Nonetheless, he was here on a personal mission. He had to locate those damn files before Det. Jarrod returned to escort him out the door. Demanding to know why he was here in the first place. This was not his case, he imagined Det. Jarrod exclaiming; tilting his head in a mysterious manner wondering what Sgt. Willowbee was up to.

Det. Jarrod had reasons not to be so trusting of his fellow officers. His partner of eleven years had been found guilty of embezzlement, police corruption, and murder. Det. Jarrod's partner had set up a known drug dealer for a police sting that wasn't on the books. Det. Jarrod's partner and three other police officers (not more than two years on the force) had fruitlessly robbed but successfully murdered a well-known drug dealer. They thought they would get away clean and no one would prosecute because they had rid the city of a known drug dealer, but that was far from the truth. It was his partner's blabbermouth that would eventually lead to his own demise. Det. Jarrod testified on behalf of his partner; the partner he thought he knew, and Det. Jarrod was disappointed when a single thumb print sealed his partner's fate. After much embarrassment, anger, and ill-feelings, Det. Jarrod finally moved passed the despicable acts of his partner and stood tall again.

Sgt. Willowbee gradually walked to the front of the desk and shuffled through Mr. Holmes desk drawers. He felt as if he was violating Mr. Holmes's again. But he didn't have time for guilt. He had to find those files and fast.

As he cautiously searched every desk drawer, he looked up in bewilderment. "I thought she said the files were in the desk drawer. Or did she say the credenza drawers? This is ridiculous," he annoyingly whispered.

He moved several feet from the desk and opened the top credenza drawer and began vigorously searching. After several frustrating heart pounding minutes, he found what he was looking for. "Now all I have to do is get these files out of here without anyone seeing me— good luck." he said to himself with little reassurance. Holding the files in his right hand, he scanned the scene with much anticipation. Anticipating Det. Jarrod would walk through the study door any moment now.

He paused…*nothing*.

He slowly walked toward the door but before he made it to the opening, he heard footsteps in the distance. All his cop confidence drifted with the breeze out an opened window in Mr. Holmes' office. He instantly panicked. Sweat started formulating on his forehead. He used the back of his right hand to wipe the sweat and noticed that he was still holding the infamous files. He released an exertive sigh and fumbled with the files, shifting them from one hand to the other. The adrenaline ran through his body like a lethal injection. He felt like a school age boy trying to hide a big secret from his parents that beat him on regular bases. He felt out of control. In a way, the situation was out of control, he thought. If he was caught holding *potential* evidence, this would be the end of his career.

The footsteps grew closer and Sgt. Willowbee was at a dilemma. He suddenly stopped in his tracks with the deer in the headlights expression, and for a fleeting moment, he froze. "Pull yourself together," he finally muttered to himself. Quickly, he pulled up his shirt and tucked the files inside his jeans and used the back-waist band of the jeans to secure the folder. He pulled his shirt down and walked out the office door. He nearly collided with one of the rookie officers on gate duty. The rookie had his head slightly tilted down in shame from the blessing out he received from Det. Jarrod regarding the commotion at the front entrance minutes earlier.

The officer nodded his head saying hello but with uncertainty and Sgt. Willowbee acknowledged the gesture. No words were exchanged—none were needed.

Sgt. Willowbee slipped out the front door, examined the windows as if he were looking for a clue, and moved swiftly across the heavy treed yard, through an old rusty broken wrought-iron fence on the side of the estate and eased onto the sidewalk toward his car. He had parked near the house next door, which was more like a half a block. Most of the homes within this respectable Bloomfield Hills neighborhood were mini mansions.

Most were over six thousand square feet. The Holmes Estate was about seventy-four hundred square feet. Why a couple with no children would purchase a home of that size was beyond Sgt. Willowbee. He didn't understand why the rich spent their money so frivolously. He didn't understand why he was under Mrs. Deveraux spell. He surely didn't understand why he panicked back there in the study. And he most certainly didn't understand why he was caught in the middle of this bloody mess.

Chapter 4

Under No Circumstances

"*ERROR IN OUR TOWN; THE BLOOMFIELD Hills Massacre; A Methodical Madman: The Serial Killer of Bloomfield Hills; A Prominent Killer on the Loose,*"— were the depicting headlines in the Detroit Newspaper and Free Press and eventually made headlines across the nation airing on CNBC. It was a nightmare for the local authorities. While the press marveled the fact that there were no leads, the Bloomfield Hills Police Department was up to its elbows in threatening phone calls and lawyer visits. Some of the most prominent people in Oakland County were being murdered in their own home and the police weren't doing enough to stop the killer, their lawyers would protest. The department was threatened with lawsuits if this madman wasn't caught by a particular time frame, their lawyers hissed.

Captain Crawford had heard all this before. One of the downsides of providing public safety service in a town where some of the most well-to-do influential people lived, you occasionally received lawsuit threats for many reasons: "—my dog should be allowed to poop and the city should have to clean it up because I pay my tax dollars – you'll be hearing from my attorney; I feel as though I am being harassed, these trees have been in my family for hundreds of years and no I will not trim them—"

But this was something altogether different, this was murder. Captain Crawford knew there would be all sort of heat on this one. He had every available man working on this case, designating a separate team of detectives to handle each crime scene. The Smits's deaths were handled by Sgt. Willowbee and Detective Margret Bridges; the Palowski's deaths were examined by Det. Jarrod and Detective Edwards; the Langdon's murder was handled by Detective Louise Popper and Detective Bridges; and the Holmes's investigation was assigned to Det. Jarrod and Detective Willington.

The plan was to assign multiple detectives to the case and they could collaborate later, but it seemed that Det. Jarrod simply took over the entire investigation. It didn't matter much to Captain Crawford; he had predicted this action. But what the Captain could not predict was the killer's next move. They had his *modus operandi* down to a *T* with no surprises except for the Holmes murder. The killer was very careful, clean, precise, and very conscientious of the time he could spend at each crime scene. The scattered papers across the floor, the messy desk, the typical uniformed look throughout the Holmes office reeked of an entirely different odor. It appeared to be the work of another perpetrator, the Captain suggested.

"Ok guys, what do we have?" Captain Crawford knowingly asked as he entered the quad room.

"Not a damn thing," a seasoned officer mumbled.

A few chuckles were faintly heard near the rear of the room but Captain Crawford didn't feel the need to address this immaterial laughter. His soured look was enough to silence the room once more.

"We really don't have a lot to go on Captain," Det. Jarrod stated.

"We got that part. I need to know what *do* you have to go on," the Captain asked with irritation.

"What we have is a travesty, that's what we have and he's in control," Sgt. Willowbee added in a stark grim voice. "We have nothing and he knows it."

"We know that he has been to each residence on more than one occasion. He was very comfortable with the layout and how much time he had to commit each murder. We know he's extremely meticulous (if we need to keep saying that) and exceedingly patient. He's invited in or forces his way into their homes (because there were no signs of a break-in or forced entry); and shoots them in the head. Usually the husband's first, then the wife. Which may indicate that the husbands knew their killer," Det. Jarrod added with certainty. "I started considering each victims' background, starting with the husbands first. Although their backgrounds were quite interesting, I have yet to come up with a solid lead. I still think that I'm on the right track Captain," he added with even more assurance.

"That's good Det. Jarrod, stay on that. What else?"

"We are still waiting for the ballistic analysis to come back from the forensic lab in Lansing," Det. Edwards added.

"Then get on their asses Edwards. I needed those reports yesterday," Captain Crawford barked.

"Will do, Captain."

"What else?"

"I believe the positioning of the bodies is going to be one of our biggest clues. The fibers that were found on the back of Mrs. Smits's blouse appeared to be consistent with the fibers found at the Langdon's mansion," Bridges added.

"Have we gotten any of these reports yet…the pathology report, trace evidence…anything?" Captain Crawford yelled. None of the detectives responded. "Come on people, I need you on the ball here. I will call the *State of Michigan Forensics Lab* tomorrow and see if I can get some headway."

"I can look into the background of Samantha Langdon. The Langdon's were one of the richest couples to be murdered so it has got to be a lengthy background there," Bridges added with a candid smile.

"Do that. But I still need you to be extremely focused on the first murder, *the Smits*," the Captain sturdily stated.

"Yes, I'm working on that as well. However, the Smits murders seem more on the religious side than the others. The only connection that ties the Smits murders to the Langdon and Palowski murders is the fact that the arms and legs were cut off each of the male Vics," Bridges stated.

"Naw…I think this is the work of the same killer," Det. Jarrod declared and then added, "so, are you suggesting that the intended target was the Smits and the rest is from a possible copycat or—"

Bridges politely interrupted, "It's a possibility. But as the victims are adding up, this may be the work of the same killer; I just didn't want to rule out the possibilities that there could be a different suspect connected to the Smits murders.

"However, I do agree that we have ourselves a serial killer on the loose in our great city. As I said, I am still looking into those strange fibers that I mentioned before; they just may be our first break. But they could turn out to be common manufactured textile fibers."

"You're right," Det. Edwards agreed.

"These crimes seem to be getting stranger by the minute. Another thing that I've noticed but it may turn out to be nothing…is that Oxford Langdon appeared to have been dead for more than a few hours. The medical examiner estimated his time of death between four and seven in the evening and yet the bodies were not discovered until eight the next morning. When we got to the scene, the blood that spilled from Mr. Langdon's body had just started to coagulate. If he had died the day before, the blood would've been dry. I sent some blood and bone fragment samples to a private forensic pathologist that owed me a favor," Bridges stated.

"Good, let's keep at it people. We've got to catch this bastard and *fast*," Captain Crawford added.

"Oh, I think I may have a break on that unusual large nail that was removed from Ronald Smits's hand," Bridges added.

"Great. Let me know what you find out."

"Oh, Captain, that brings me to my other dilemma that we discussed…"

Captain Crawford cut her off and responded, "…No, no, no…we are not going to question Mrs. Deveraux unless it is absolutely necessary. Sgt. Willowbee and I have had a long history with Mrs. Deveraux and we need to handle that one like eggshells. *Under no circumstances will she be questioned without my knowledge,*" he implacably added.

"But Captain…"

"Under *no* circumstances, Bridges."

"Ok, ok. I still think that she's hiding something," Bridges added shrugging her shoulders.

"She's always hiding something," Sgt. Willowbee added nauseatingly.

"Tell me about it," Captain Crawford silently agreed. "Ok guys let's get back to work. Let's make something happen by the end of the day and I don't mean another murdered victim." He smashed his hands together in one motion and shouted once more, "Let's go, let's go…we need to find this asshole and fast."

"I STILL DON'T get why the Captain is treating this woman as if she was the president," Bridges said to Sgt. Willowbee.

"Just let it go Bridges. You couldn't possibly understand. Mrs. Deveraux is relentless," Sgt. Willowbee replied.

"Try me." her voice filled with anticipation.

"It's a long story. All you need to know is that the last time we *simply* indicated that Mrs. Deveraux *could be* involved in corrupt business practices she nearly owned the Bloomfield Hills Police Department. She showed us just how powerful she could be."

"That doesn't give her *a ticket to murder,*" Bridges added infuriatingly.

"Yes, we know. But we've got to play it smart this time. If she's involved, it'll surface. We've really got to be smart about this one." Sgt. Willowbee stared straight ahead in a daze. Eyes fixated on nothing. The teary glare that covered his pupils showed the magnitude of his deep trance.

"Sgt. Willowbee?"

No response— just a still glare that paralyzed his thoughts. He heard a muttered sound in the distance but was unable to unlock the grasp of his reverie.

"Sergeant, are you okay," Bridges nervously asked.

Without looking toward her, he responded, "Yeah, I'm okay." And without any thing further, he pulled the black unmarked police cruiser from the curb and headed to the Smits residence again, in hopes of retrieving a clue that they may have missed the last two times before.

THE BRUTAL NIGHT air contrasted sharply with the grace of the Smits' mansion on Willow Creek Drive just on the outskirts of a newly constructed subdivision of less expensive homes. The Smits family was what you would call *old money*. Ronald Smits inherited his wealth from his father's fortune which was passed down several generations from their great, great grandfather Odie Smits.

Although it was obvious that there were no signs of life inside the mansion and the yellow crime scene tape hugged around the immaculate French doors; the mansion was still breathtaking.

Bridges and Sgt. Willowbee maneuvered under the tape and entered the home. The cathedral type ceilings were enough to steal your breath away. The strainer arches of ogee curves were remarkably sculpted and designed with such precision. The fan-vaulted ceilings were twenty feet high with a hand painted mural of *The Last Supper* and the beveled stained glass that was uniquely structured to form a portrait of Jesus floating in the background.

The Smits were a highly religious family and Bridges skeptically wondered how they tied into all this. What they could have done to deserve such a vicious death, she thought.

"Why were they the first? What are we going to find here today?" she mischievously asked, gently sliding her hands together as if she was on *The Price Is Right* and she was asked to select the door that harbored the brand-new car.

"My guess is nothing," Sgt. Willowbee said.

"They'll speak to us; we simply have to know where to look," Bridges added.

"I must say that we've got some of the most thorough crime scene investigators in the country dissecting these crime scenes."

"But did they *thoroughly* analyze *this* crime scene? They were the first couple to be murdered and we didn't realize that we had a psycho serial killer on our hands until the second murder," she said matter-of-factly.

"No, our local boys analyzed this scene," he said unwittingly. He glanced at Bridges who had an undefeated smirk across her face and added, "Ok, so they may not have *dissected* this house but they are pretty thorough as well."

"I'm sure they are but let's just have a look around, shall we."

"After you." He motioned his hand with a slight bow of his head and insisted that she lead the way. Sgt. Willowbee followed behind Bridges, eyes rolled and skepticism planted on his face.

Bridges is a hot-headed red head. She's the department's wild card. She's easily excited, very ambitious, and outlandish in her behavior; which gave her an advantage when it came to dismembering strange cases such as these. She is known for disobeying orders and had gotten use to Captain Crawford threatening suspension. It didn't faze her any; she usually went with her gut and it was usually correct. While she is known to be correct most the time, this didn't earn her respect from her peers. Three years as an officer wasn't enough time to be certain, thought Sgt. Willowbee. Nonetheless, she was good at her job and she didn't care if she was admired or appreciated. She wanted to solve this crime. Not for the fame or glory but for the satisfaction that she had done her job and she had performed it well.

Bridges didn't need to be a detective. She was born and raised in Bloomfield Hills, Michigan. Saying that would suggest that she was born into a wealthy family. Her father was a doctor and her mother was a lawyer – typical hardworking parents with even bigger dreams for their daughter. Even though their home was one of the few modest homes in Bloomfield Hills, they still carried themselves with the utmost sophistication. Rumor has it that Bridges' mother was born into wealth but disobeyed her father by going to law school. *"Stubbornness that Bridges inherited, I'm sure,"* Captain Crawford once stated to Sgt. Willowbee when he had asked why Bridges wouldn't let things go. Bridges' grandfather wanted her mother to help with the family business— which Bridges' had not discovered, even today, what the family business was because her mother never talked about it.

Bridges had masterfully done the same as her mother; she had disobeyed her parents' orders and dropped out of college in her junior year and became a police officer. She argued that she knew the city and the surrounding cities better than anyone in Bloomfield Hills. Surprisingly, this argument had some truth to it. Bridges did know the respecting streets of Bloomfield Hills,

Berkeley, most of Detroit, and parts of Oakland and Wayne county relatively well.

Despite the unfavorable outcome of Bridges' life, thought her parents; she had successfully climbed up the ranks to Lead Detective in only three years. Some say it was her mother's wealth that brought her this far; others say it was out of respect for her father who was admired by the community; and a handful realized from day one (including Captain Crawford) that she was something special. She had it, whatever *it* was, she had it. She was good at her job and she knew it.

Even after her parents unexpected death in a car accident, she still wanted to maintain her sensible lifestyle. So, when she discovered that her mother had a twenty-four million dollar trust fund in her name that would transfer to Bridges upon her mother's death, she anonymously donated the entire trust fund to charity.

Of course, some of the boys at the station still believe she's rich and hence their disrespect toward Bridges. They continue to question why she's here and what she's trying to prove. "Damn crybabies," she would say.

Bridges kneeled down and calmly brushed her hands across the travertine floor in the master bathroom. "Why were you found in this spot Mrs. Smits?" she whispered in wonder. "You weren't with your husband at first— you ran up here to hide after you witnessed the killer shoot Mr. Smits. Why are you mixed up in all of this?" She slowly stood up from the floor and glanced across the bathroom with intriguing eyes; leaving no area missed. "There's got to be something here," she stated.

"Something like what?" Sgt. Willowbee asked.

"I don't know. Ok, let's try to reconstruct the scene— the killer comes in and shoot Mr. Smits, right. But Mrs. Smits is doing something else; perhaps getting ready for dinner and she is unaware of the commotion downstairs. She hears the first shot or a strange sound coming from the living area and strolls to the top of the stairs to call for her husband…"

Sgt. Willowbee interrupts but pleasantly, "Ok, I follow."

"…the killer hears her or notices her at the top of the stairs and realizes that he must kill her too. He has already killed Mr. Smits. Mr. Smits is lying in the middle of the floor, in a pool of his own blood and dying slowly…or he's already dead. The killer rushes across the room, travels up the stairs and finds Mrs. Smits hovering over the toilet. He executes her with one shot in the middle of the forehead. Execution style. Without batting an eye, he drags her body to the middle of the bathroom floor and neatly positions her body as if he was making her comfortable or posing her for a portrait. The blood and brain matter splattered on the wall was a good indication that she was shot sitting up next to the toilet and not as she lay on the floor. Why? Why would he reposition her body? What was that all about…?"

"So many questions and so little answers," Sgt. Willowbee stated.

Still deep in thought, Bridges narrowed her eyes and said, "The answer is in this house; I can feel it."

Chapter 5

Beyond Power

RONALD WAS PULLED FROM HIS STUDY BY A clacking noise. Maybe a galloping noise, he thought. He removed his body from his leather chair where he sat cozy next to a small symmetrical marble table, reading a *Eldredge* book by the intimation of light from the small table lamp, and headed toward the front of the house. Ideally, he had thought it was his wife moving about the floor in her high heel shoes as she was getting ready to leave for bible study. This seemingly natural idea was challenged when Mrs. Deveraux walked through his office door.

"Hello Mr. Smits," Mrs. Deveraux pleasantly said.

"Well, hello, Mrs. Deveraux. And what can I do for you today," he said with a puzzled expression across his face.

"I just love the intriguing look of your home. It reminds me of my days in church. And those ceilings are splendid," she said with sarcasm but surprisingly believable. With a refined eloquence, she stated, "It has come to my attention that you own a share in the rugged eye sore that sits on the west end of Detroit. I don't know if you are aware but there are several people that share an interest in that property, including myself.

"I suppose I'll be blunt Mr. Smits; I would like to make you an offer for your share. It isn't really a valuable piece of property and my intentions may very well go beyond the scope of my abilities; nonetheless, I want to buy your share. I have great plans for the land not the building." She floated across the office as if she had been there before; displacing books, admiring paintings as if she was enjoying a daily content view. She adjusted the office chair to have a seat and patiently awaited Mr. Smits's response but boastfully knew a favorable one was forthcoming.

"Thank you for the compliment of my home. But, I must say, I am rather surprised that you have come to me. My share is purely a fraction. *Surely*…you have not forgotten who owns a share of the building and land," Smits said sharply.

"I am well aware of your current court situation with the Grimshaw Estate. I have also been made aware of your intent to coerce me into forwarding my portion of the investment. You know very well that I am aware of the parties involved. It seems that Grimshaw, you and I have an interest in this property and land; however, Mr. Grimshaw has been missing for over 15 years. You have managed to take over most of his fortune (after the state declared him dead nine years ago), and effacing any inheritance that his family was entitled to; and now, this *one* piece of investment would arise your richly desire. Why?" Smits tugged for a response from Mrs. Deveraux, but none was given, so he continued, "It seems this investment is of inestimable value to you, Mrs. Deveraux. But my question is simple, would this sincerely satisfy you or would your greed starve for more?" he candidly stated. Removed an imported cigar from a uniquely crafted cigar box, massaged it between his fingertips, clipped the end and light it with much delight.

"Well, well, well Mr. Smits. You certainly have done your homework," she said with a wide smile. "I marvel at the fact that you consider yourself a highly religious man and yet you have drenched your mind in gossip. Shame, shame, shame Mr. Smits." She smiled and slowly lifted herself from the office chair. "I never did like that picture of me in the paper. It didn't capture my best side, would you say." she playfully said.

"It appalls me how you find this amusing Mrs. Deveraux. You seem to be getting some form of intoxicating pleasure from this little charade, so I will save us both some dignity and be as blunt as you— *no*. I will not consider your offer and do have every intention on seeing this project through. We originally set out to build a much-needed apartment complex for moderate income families and somehow, we lost sight of that. As long as I have a breath in my body, you will not burn out another family. You don't leave much to desire about you Mrs. Deveraux, your character screams through your money."

"Oh you have no idea what my character can do, Mr. Smits." She moved in closer to Mr. Smits, rested her bottom on the edge of his executive desk, leaned in close to his ear and repeated in a provocative whisper that assaulted your senses, "You have no idea what my character can do, Mr. Smits." A sense of evil twirled inside your stomach and the verge of darkness manifested inside your soul. An eruption of power enveloped you as you were forced to concede.

Mrs. Deveraux walked back toward the neat rows of displayed books on the wall and said matter-of-factly, "You may be correct about one thing, my money does scream – *loudly*. And I am trying to give it away. Now what does that say for my character?"

"Keep your money, it's more becoming to you."

"Well, Mr. Smits, I am sorry you feel that way." She released a hefty sigh, smiled, and then continued, "Nevertheless, I still would like to address my proposal if I may."

"Your proposal has been heard and denied," he said meekly.

"You are a gracious man. A man of God," she faintly laughed. "Oh how I wish I had your humility."

"Is there anything further that I can assist you with, Mrs. Deveraux?"

"As a matter-of-fact there is..."

"Good day Mrs. Deveraux. I think our discussion has come to an eventful end." He pushed back from the desk and stood up.

"Please, Mr. Smits, have a seat. I have one more thing to run by you. *Please.*" She said sternly. "It will only take a few more minutes of your time and off to church you go."

He cautiously smirked and slowly lowered his bottom back inside the plush suede executive office chair he had moved to upon Mrs. Deveraux's arrival. The next intensified moments seemed like hours had passed by. Mr. Smits sat in wonder, trying to anticipate the unexpected. His heart started small thrust of irregular beating. His hand perspired within the palm that held his imported cigar. He stammered over his next thought. Despite the calm confident appearance, he was starting to unfold inside, but with a strong effort, he slightly recovered and prepared himself for Mrs. Deveraux's iniquitous thrashing.

WITH MUCH HESITATION, Ronald signed the papers that Mrs. Deveraux handed him. A Quitclaim Deed which relinquished his rights to the building and land. And with such delicacy, she intimately folded the papers in half and inserted them inside a manila folder.

"Of course, you're thinking that I am an evil person." Mrs. Deveraux paused, glanced over at Mr. Smits through the corner of her eyes and continued, "But the truth is I'm much worse than you could ever imagine, Mr. Smits. I have come so far in my endeavors and I will not stop at a minor infraction. I will do whatever is necessary to reach my goals."

"Assuming your goal is to win at the expense of others."

"On the contrary, Mr. Smits...at my own expense. I told you that I was making you an offer. I have already transferred fifty thousand dollars into your account for your *fraction* of the land. Everything's perfectly legal. I tried to cover all the bases, did I miss anything?" she said mordantly.

"If you think you're going to get away with this you are sadly mistaken," he replied with fury.

"Such a cliché Mr. Smits— let's try to think of other, more suited words, shall we," she said with grave disappointment.

"You will not get away with this Mrs. Deveraux."

"I already have," she replied. She stood up from the office chair, pasted her footsteps to the door and added, "Don't mess with me Mr. Smits. I have been overly kind to you because I respect you and in a strange sort-of-way, I like you. I admire what you stand for— righteousness. But please don't misunderstand my kindness. I will stop at nothing, Mr. Smits, please remember that," she profoundly stated.

HE TURNED THE key to unlock the door. With the click of the lock, he felt cold metal placed at his temple. He instantly froze. The perpetrator whispered something but Ronald didn't hear it. After several undeniably long seconds with his hand gripping the doorknob and sweat building inside the palm of his hand, he refocused. His mind had clearly identified what was happening but his soul had denied its irrefutable observation. He soon felt the barrel of the pistol dig deep into his flesh.

"I said move it Mr. Smits," the assailant angrily whispered once more.

Fearing the unknown he tried to stall at the front entrance while he struggled for a conspicuous thought.

Nothing. "What do you want," Ronald managed to mutter.

"Don't make me say it again, Mr. Smits."

"I don't keep money in the house but I do have about thirty-four hundred dollars in my wallet. You can have it; it's yours," he nervously declared. "Lord...please don't hurt me. Whatever the problem is, I'm sure we can work something out.

"Your fate has already been decided Mr. Smits. Please, *stop stalling dammit*," the assailant whispered again through his tight teeth.

Even his final leap of faith didn't appeal to the perpetrator. Ronald unwillingly opened the door, shoving it hard enough, in an effort to create a disturbance. His deploy didn't work, Debra (his wife) had moved the console for this very reason. *One day you will slam that door right into this table and all my plants will go flying across the floor*, she would say. "Damn," he thought to himself, begging the Lord's forgiveness for the abrupt curse word.

Then suddenly, he stood taller, he turned incrementally to face his assailant, and his heart stopped throbbing. His conscious became clearer. A splendid smile drifted in place. He knew he was already home, even before he heard the gunshot blast. "I pray my wife is unharmed," he whispered a fraction of a second before the blast and a second before his body hit the mahogany hardwood floor, bounced once on his back and ended slightly twisted onto his side and stomach.

The gunshot echoed unmercifully throughout the cathedral style ceilings, bouncing from wall-to-wall. Debra – Mrs. Smits – had recently returned from her bible study class, made her way upstairs, and had just started to undress. She got as far has her heels, when she heard a commotion. It sounded more like a man staggering in drunk, she thought. She knew it couldn't have been her Ronald. He had not had a drink in over five years. He had been sober for more than seven years. "It must be Ronald messing around down there," she casually whispered, although she could not place the loud piercing sound that lingered through the air after the commotion.

She started unbuttoning her blouse as she strolled to the staircase. She peeked over the railing and shock embraced her face. She saw the killer suspended over her husband with intensity. Her mild gasp caught his attention. His head jerked back as if his body had been yanked from the trance. He stumbled and headed toward the stairs. He ran upstairs after Mrs. Smits. Mrs. Smits was horrified. Her body was shackled from the restraints of terror. She couldn't move. She had not thought that the darkness would fall on her so soon, but she released a quaint sigh and exhaled softly, just before the killer gripped the trigger with mad force. Her head went limp as her body slumped over to the left.

The killer watched the blood ease from her open wound. The sight of blood always restrained him. His eyes were drawn to the blood that gradually moved down the victim's face. It was like he was watching a puzzling movie unfold. He was mesmerized.

Unaffected by the death slipping woman he was fixated on; the killer's mind had suddenly been gripped by the demons that controlled him. He tried to curb the evil that lay inside of him but the compulsion was too great.

After shooting Mrs. Smits, he ran downstairs and dismembered Mr. Smits body and neatly positioned Mr. Smits's arms and legs beside his torso. The killer would reposition their bodies before leaving through one of the back doors.

Chapter 6

The Voice of Blackmail

THE DISTINGUISHING FEATURES OF MRS. Deveraux were taunting and unforgettable. However, she was one of the most ravishing women in Bloomfield Hills, perhaps in Oakland county. It was easy to engulf yourself in her tantalizing features: her mysteriously long dark hair; those captivating hazelnut eyes; her boldly heart shaped face; that magnetic stare; her sensuous potty lips; her voluptuous twenty-five-year-old figure that would make any man's heart skip a beat when she walked by. Her provocative allure, meant to tease and disturb your senses, was only a hint of her riveting nature. Nevertheless, her dangerous coldhearted demeanor obscured your vision and your intriguing thoughts melted away like butter.

Believe it or not, Mrs. Deveraux saw all these features staring back at her while she stood in the master bathroom mirror. She knew her appearance was much to be desired. She knew her coldness was an art that she had mastered over the years. She also knew, without a doubt, that she was one of the most powerful women in the state of Michigan and she had only just begun.

She tested the water with the tips of her fingers. It was scorching hot, just as she had wanted it to be. Nearly burning off her skin was how it should feel, she thought. She often retreated to her sanctuary in search of relaxation. A hot bath usually did it for her. She engulfed her body in the baking hot water and melted away her frustrations. She used this time to reflect on her emotions; and each night she would find herself asking the same question, "How did I become so unattached to myself, to life?" Somewhere deep inside her heart was a darkened place and a deep hole that nothing or no one could fulfill. She knew this. No matter how much money she had or how miserable she would make someone else's life, it wasn't enough.

She needed her soaking time to reflect on how empty she felt and how she masqueraded behind a mask that no one had managed to see through, not even her husband of twenty-three years. This was a heavy kept secret that she vowed to carry to her grave.

Each night she would soak in the tub for at least a half-hour. Periodically, however, her husband would find the most perfect inapt time to interrupt her moment of enchantment.

Ring, ring.

"What is it dear," she said releasing a heavy sigh.

"I just called to let you know that I would not be home tonight," he stated.

"Why?" she sang with little concern.

"I have a meeting that ran over and tomorrow I must fly to Miami to straighten out this deal before it falls through." His voice seemed more shaken than usual but she didn't want to dwell on it because frankly, she didn't care. He had interrupted her moment and he could have said the house was on fire and she wouldn't have been any more excited.

"Please tell me you have something more. Please tell me that you did not call me at this hour to say you wouldn't be home. What time is it Clayton?" she hissed through the phone.

"Oh dear, I simply didn't make note of the time. I'm terribly sorry," he said apologetically.

"You damn right you're sorry."

Click.

Without warning, she firmly pressed end on her cell phone and tossed the phone across the master bathroom into a cozy chair. She rubbed her fingers through her hair, emerged her body deeper in the tub of water, and relaxed her neck on the edge of the tub. She closed her eyes and for the next half an hour, she lay in silence.

Ring, ring. The sounds of her 50's telephone ring came roaring through the air from across the room. "If that is Clayton again..." she angrily alleged.

She stepped out of the tub, gently toweled her body dry, and walked over to check her missed calls. To her surprise, it wasn't her husband. Mrs. Deveraux didn't recognize the number.

"If it's that important, they'll phone again." After several minutes her phone rang again. "Hello," she said sharply. Giving the late hour—ten thirty-two in the evening—she was not in the mood for conversation.

"Hello Mrs. Deveraux," an unknown voice softly said.

"Who is this?" she asked abruptly.

"Who I am is of no importance right now but what I know is," he stated in a charming voice. She could feel the unknown voice smiling through the phone.

"What could possibly be so important this time of night? Who is this?" she hissed again.

"Ok, if it relaxes your tongue, you can call me Tom."

"*Tom.* Can this conversation wait until the morning Tom?"

"I'm afraid not," he said with enthusiasm.

She gently wiped her damp cheeks with the tip of the drying towel. She contemplated on her next response but was too tired to play the game. "Look Tom, I'm afraid this will *have* to wait until the morning. This is my time and no one interrupts it."

Click.

Ring, ring.

"He simply will not give up," she whispered, and then she answered the phone on the second ring. *"What can I do for you?"* she said sharply.

"I know all about you Mrs. Deveraux," he said in a whisper.

Silence.

"I know what you did—manipulating Mr. Smits into signing those corrupt documents. Shame on you Mrs. Deveraux. But this isn't your first time. You've done this before. If history serves me correctly, you were being investigated several years back for forging documents. Presenting fraudulent documents to the court contesting your majority interest in property and land that wasn't legally yours, does that sound about right Mrs. Deveraux," he said matter-of-factly.

Still, Mrs. Deveraux did not respond.

"I'll take your silence as a yes," he added.

"What do you want," she managed to say. Distress dismantled her face but she desperately tried to conceal it. Her voice was unnoticeably scratchy and she could feel her hand tremble as she held the phone to her ear in disbelief. Who could have possibly seen or heard her, she thought. Mr. Smits is dead so it was obvious that he wasn't talking. Who is this strange character on the other end of her phone, she wondered.

"I've got to keep him talking," she thought to herself.

"Your natural reaction would be to offer me a settlement for what I know. But an exact amount hasn't crossed your mind at this time because you have no idea as to the extent of my knowledge. You're probably trying to concoct an elaborate scheme to keep me talking and possibly reveal myself to you so you would have control of the situation. I'm sure I'm right or at least in the ball park of what you were thinking but you would never admit that, isn't that right Mrs. Deveraux.

"You know, Mrs. Deveraux seems so formal, can I call you Julie Ann?" You could feel his smile widen through the phone. It stretched across Oakland county and parts of Wayne county too.

"Do not think you know me or what I'm thinking. Make your point quick, I'm getting restless," she said, in a deep warm controlled voice, trying hard to maintain her composure.

"I'm just playing your game. Oh, I get it. Since the ball isn't in your court, and the cameras are fixated on another player, you don't want to participate anymore. Well, it doesn't work like that Julie Ann. But for the time being, I'll state my claim: meet me at the legendary partially constructed abandon building that everyone seems to have a stake in tomorrow night at seven thirty. Don't be late Julie…"

She cut off his last words and said, "Don't call me Julie Ann. That's Mrs. Deveraux to you." The line went silent. She pulled the phone away from her ear and saw her wallpaper staring back at her. He had hung up. She explicitly worried away at this dilemma. The shoe was on the other foot and she didn't know how to handle it. No one had ever trampled over her feet before. No one dared to question her, let alone threaten her with blackmail. This was absurd, she thought. She wondered if it was a joke but he knew too much for this to be a hoax. At this point, she felt she had no choice; she had to meet him at the abandon construction site.

FOR THE FIRST time in thirty years Mrs. Deveraux slept restless, if she slept at all. Anticipating what the day would bring was enough excitement to keep her eyes wide open during the night. She studied the clock intensely, waiting for six p.m. It was daunting.

Mrs. Deveraux traveled down Eight Mile Road, circled around the island (a Michigan left) to turn right onto Lasher Road. A block down on the right was an abandon construction site. Two CAT equipment trucks sat deep in the weeded soul. It had been over nine years since she had visited the site. She pulled into a partially laid concrete opening that stopped just at the front of the unfinished building. She briefly looked through her car windows to survey the area. The dark clouds in the sky hinted at a storm. They briskly roamed across the infant building. Her eyes shined unsteadily and the thunder roared like a stalwart lion. And in that instant, she could feel that eerie feeling she felt yesterday while on the phone with *Tom*.

She sensed a slight hesitation as she fought with her fear to exit her vehicle. But on the other hand, it was her peculiar curiosity that overpowered her fright. She had anticipated this meeting of the minds.

Since he had obviously done some homework on her, her ripples of fear had turned into inquisitiveness. She grinned at the prospect of seeing him froth at the mouth and jolting for the door after she sunk her teeth into his neck with massive force. This thought produced a wide smile. In the middle of a satisfying thought, her phone rang.

"You're used to being luxuriated in riches and emotionally withdrawn from the poverty that surrounds your Bloomfield city. You have no idea how these people live over here, do you Julie Ann?" the caller on the other end stated.

"Where are you?" she said, while scanning the area.

"I am exactly where I need to be, in a delicate position. Well, delicate for you Julie Ann. I contemplated on going to the police with this information but I figured you would simply wiggle your way out of it. You would manipulate Sgt. Willowbee; expose the department's little secrets and threaten with another lawsuit. Hell, with your connections you could very well own the police, you probably already do," he said with sureness.

Her heart started racing but not with fear, with anger. She became infuriated the more Tom spoke. "So, you think you have discovered my frailties. Listen here you piece-of-shit, no one threatens me or attempt to humiliate me by counting my *so-called* unprincipled actions on their fingertips. Despite your charming demeanor and friendly disposition over the phone, you are just like me. If you wanted to go to the police you would have done so by now. If you gave a shit about the people that live in this god-awful neighborhood, this building wouldn't be up for debate. You would have turned this eye sore into something more useful to the community. But it has sat here, unfinished, for fifteen years. Now, get to the point because I'm finished playing this game with you. I've been at this a lot longer than you Sweetie and you are way out of your element young man." Her powerful voice echoed through the phone and a frightful energy consumed Tom's body.

You could hear the lump in his throat swallow hard. He anticipated her harsh tone but he didn't realize how piercing her words would be. He had heard the rumors and read her profile, but nothing would properly prepare him for today. He stuttered for a moment in silence before quickly pulling himself together. His voice noticeably coarse, "I don't want your money—"

"Then what *do* you want Mr. Tom. If that is your real name, assuming it's not, but for the sake of communicating, what is it that you could possibly want besides money, *Tom*?"

"I want you and all that you have to be *dissolved*."

Click.

Chapter 7

Business as Usual

MEANWHILE, THE CRUEL AND FEARSOME MRS. Deveraux had went on with plans as usual. Ironically, Mrs. Deveraux had theorized that this day would come where her power would be challenged. A subtle smile drifted in position when she thought of Tom, and then a malevolence plan forged. She needed an impeccable scheme to fish out Tom. She had to know who belonged to the voice on the other end of the receiver. She thought of an unmatched plan but didn't have time to consider it suddenly. She remembered she had a meeting with Mitch Cooper of *Cooper Construction and Excavation Company,* which she was now late for.

"You're late again Mrs. Deveraux and this project is late as well," Mr. Cooper barked as she drove up next to him at an unknown construction site.

"Well, Mr. Cooper, I see your panties are in a bunch this afternoon."

"I had my boys waiting at that damn location for over two hours and you didn't even bother to show up. Do you know how much those two hours cost me? I had twelve men on duty that day—"

Before he could complete his sentence, "Oh Mr. Cooper; stop your whining. I told you that this project would continue as originally planned. I just have a few wrinkles to iron out. Please, be patient. I have paid you a nice sum of money to get this project off and running so don't give me that insignificant bullshit about how much money you had to pay your workers. I am paying you handsomely for the completion of this project, so don't misunderstand our agreement. We have agreed that you would build my dream masterpiece, *not run it or me.* You move when I say move, not when *you* feel it is appropriate. If you can't handle that Mr. Cooper, I can very well find someone else who would be more than eager to accommodate."

He fixed his eyes on her movements while she eloquently stepped out of her 750Li BMW. For a brief moment, he thought of how beautiful she looked. Her graceful slender legs, that could stop a tracker trailer in motion, slipped out of the vehicle with such refinement. The ivory skirt suit that hugged her curvy body manipulated a glow in your eyes. And her ivory three quarter length suit jacket that accompanied the skirt suit blew through the air with a velvet touch.

Even as she blurted her crude intimidation—sharp and swift; after she beckoned for him to concede; after her voice penetrated his ears with fright—he still couldn't be more blown away by her gripping features. Her baby smooth skin and her warm-felt leer captured his attention and the attention of most of the labor workers. But this musing only lasted for a *brief* moment.

Mr. Cooper didn't want or need to push Mrs. Deveraux's buttons. She was very powerful and she *could* and *would* see to it that you never worked in her city again or any surrounding cities. Not mentioning that Cooper needed this job to stay afloat.

Mrs. Deveraux paid him thirty-six thousand dollars of *front money* (to prepare the plans and obtain the permits). Their mediocre arrangement was for Mrs. Deveraux to pay him nine hundred thousand dollars to start the project and then another seven would be paid once the project was underway. Pennies, he thought, for the size of this development but he was in a bind and Mrs. Deveraux was his only way out.

Cooper Construction was on its last leg. He was going under. He had debt well over nine hundred thousand dollars and Mrs. Deveraux was not aware that the money she gave him for a down payment had nearly vanished. The nine hundred thousand dollars should have been used to cover the *soft cost* of the preliminary part of the construction project: engineering and architectural fees, surveying costs, legal fees, inspection and testing cost. Instead, he used the money to buy some time with his creditors.

But putting nine hundred thousand dollars on a three-million-dollar debt was not going to cut it with his creditors. They wanted their money yesterday. Cooper was desperate. No one knew just how desperate he was.

"I HAVEN'T REALLY been following your court saga but I suspect it has not reached a favorable decision or I would be working on a project that should be in its completion stage by now," William Kensington hissed.

"I'm offended, you don't have any faith in me." Mrs. Deveraux stated with much amuse.

"It's not you that I don't have faith in my dear, it's this project. I don't think it will happen. I have put in a lot of man hours on this deal and if it fell through I would surely be disappointed," he added notably.

He briefly pulled the phone from his ear, covered the receiver with a delicate motion of his hand, whispered something to an unknown person in the background and refocused his attention to Mrs. Deveraux and continued,

"I simply have reservation about this project coming full circle."

"Of course it will. I always get my way," she firmly stated then added, "I will not stop until this project is completed."

"I believe that. You are a determined woman and your history has proved that you can swindle your way out of anything," he said with sureness.

"Yes, that is true if you want to put it like that. I will agree that I am determined and very persuasive." She laughed and moved on to irrelevant chatter.

But Kensington wasn't ready to move on, "But we have permits in place, a timeline to focus on and many other aspects that must be considered. If this project is not underway within a few months, we'll have to reapply or ask for extensions with the city of Detroit. And you know applying for extensions and reapplying for permits means more money spent. Money and time."

"Yes, you're correct. Please don't worry Mr. Kensington, I just have a few more wrinkles to iron out and we will be all set. Trust me on this."

William Kensington is a very powerful man. Almost as powerful as Mrs. Deveraux, so she had grown to respect him more than any others. Although his business practices were more honest than Mrs. Deveraux's, he was once accused of embezzlement from a former business partner. It turned out that Mr. Cooper had understated his finances and Uncle Sam caught up with him. He tried to blame his "miscalculations" on his business dealings with Kensington but all Kensington's finances were in perfect order, according to the Forensic Accountant that was hired by the prosecutor. But the case never made it to court. Mr. Cooper's concession of guilt forced the IRS to demand a payment of over two hundred thirty thousand dollars to cover the back taxes owed and applicable fees. Money that Mr. Cooper didn't have and this was the start of his downfall.

Nevertheless, Kensington practiced fair dealings and that was another aspect that Mrs. Deveraux admired. Kensington was nearly as rich as Mrs. Deveraux, but his callused palms revealed the source of his wealth. After twenty-four years of scrambling to establish his name, Kensington was finally genteel, accomplished, and highly respected in his business and community.

After studying aboard, he came back to the States educated, articulate, and with a strong lust for life. But after his fantasy dwindled, and the bills start piling up, he decided to join the family business. It really wasn't much of a business but it was all they had.

His father, a small-time businessman who worked hard for a living and a mother who educated herself enough to keep the finances in order, had started a small town real estate business. His parents lived modestly on a hundred thousand dollars a year—on a good year.

Now, the Kensington Estate is worth more than six billion dollars. He turned his father's real estate development business into a patented empire. The *Kensington Suites*—a luxurious hotel with fine dining and exquisite catered services. His grand hotels were built with the refinement of a prominent country house like the *Waddesdon Manor* in England with its French Renaissance architecture and its 18th century Italian statues on display in front of the building that housed *Kensington Suites* headquarters. The historical lamp post that created a sparkling reflection in the shallow water that surrounded the statues had a sedative glow that lit up the front entrance.

Of course, this scene would be much too eloquent for Detroit's taste, so Kensington had an idea for a more urbanized, modern architectural concept that would incorporate the prominent feel of high society. It would still have all the elements that Mrs. Deveraux admired, which was extremely important to her. "I want the new city to take your breath away," she once said.

This was the idea that Mrs. Deveraux sought for her rough building and land. She wanted to develop a fancy hotel, fine dining, a boardwalk, and an entire community that extended beyond the parcel of land in question.

Her project would cost seventy-five million dollars and climbing. She was battling over the rights to the building and land on Lasher Road but her partners had no idea that she had purchased *all* the land from Evergreen Road to West Grand River Ave; from Nine Mile Road to Seven Mile Road—an eleven mile stretch that would soon become *The Broadway* in the new city of Wylie right outside of Detroit.

ALLURE 'DE CHAMPAIGN was an exquisite affluent restaurant in *The Mansions of Bloomfield Hills*. It was owned by *T. Robert Wesley & Company*, a sophisticated restaurant pioneer in European cuisine in the United States. Mrs. Deveraux had tried on multiple occasions to entice Wesley with her enchanting garden of eve she was planning for the new city but Wesley wasn't impressed.

"I don't think it would work Mrs. Deveraux. You do have high hopes but too high, I'm afraid. That is simply not the appropriate neighborhood for one of my restaurants. It simply wouldn't work," Wesley stated with admiration.

"I know the neighborhood is unfavorable now but it will soon be a place where people can walk the streets again. Just imagine: enjoying a superb candle lit dinner, going for a stroll across the boardwalk, in-all of the fragile garden and subtle wind that tickle your nose. Your senses are compelled to tour each store that you casually stroll by before retiring for the night at the *Kensington Suites*."

"Still…my restaurant doesn't fit into that kind of atmosphere. I am truly sorry Mrs. Deveraux, but I'm afraid that that would not work. The area is much too coarse for my taste," he said contritely.

"Oh, Mr. Wesley, what will I have to do to persuade you to come aboard this project? Your presence alone would make this project well worth the investment. I am looking to make one point two billion within the first fiscal year. Right in the heart of my land will be the remarkable downtown Wylie. The surrounding elements would be several high-class condos ranging from five hundred thousand to over two million dollars—"

"Two million, in that neighborhood," he interrupted with faint laughter and continued, "I'm afraid that would be a mere fantasy Mrs. Deveraux."

"Yes, two million. Do you know who would pay that price to live there?" she asked a rhetorical question and didn't hold for a response. "The execs from the new corporate office of *SoftLine Technologies*, that's who." she stated matter-of-factly.

"*SoftLine*—"

"Yes, *SoftLine*. And do you know how much their executives gross—somewhere in the ball park of one point five to over ten million dollars annually," she said smiling with glee.

"Umm—"

"*SoftLine* is a Fortune 100 company with estimated revenue of three hundred billion dollars, annually. Their new corporate office is moving from Tennessee to Michigan. Because of the rough economy, the tax incentives have shifted a lot of interest to the Detroit Metropolitan areas. The mediocre prices of land have aided them in their endeavors as well. The Mayor of Detroit offered *SoftLine* tax cuts for the next five years and *SoftLine* has also agreed to employ over three hundred people from the city. Their eleven thousand square foot building is at its infancy as we speak. It plans to open in the fall of 2011. I plan to have my project completed before then."

"Fall…of next year? That is impossible Mrs. Deveraux."

"Nothing is impossible. I have the permits, the backing, and the means to get it done, Mr. Wesley," she said with much certainty.

"I know that you are a very powerful woman in this city but isn't that a little presumptuous of you to assume everything is going to go your way at the court hearing?" he proclaimed. Her court troubles made headlines and every well-to-do in Bloomfield Hills read the daily paper. While they didn't always read the stories that were featured in the paper; they most certainly read the headlines and the floating roamers took care of the story.

"No, it's not. This is simply a mere formality, Mr. Wesley. I already own the land and there is no one alive to contest that. I only have fifteen months to complete this project. I plan to have the boardwalk, the condos and the transportation in place by the time *SoftLine* completes its project. There will be minor construction thereafter, but I'm sure that the executives will be too busy to complain.

"But…I must say…with the recession many companies are downsizing in order to increase productivity and maximize profits, *starting with their executives*. You don't think that this heavy financial project of *SoftLine* will weigh on their company's bottom line?"

"I've thought of that and my research concurs with my gut feeling. Their executives had an intensive meeting in early 2009 to discuss this very issue. They developed a simple but rather unique plan that would save the company money and ensure their positions at *SoftLine*. They proposed that each executive take a seven to sixteen percent pay cut on their annual salary, totaling over five million dollars. The executives that were due for retirement – *retired* – and the others agreed to the decrease of their annual salary which saved the company around thirteen million dollars within the second quarter of 2009. Pretty brilliant, I thought." She smiled a boastful smile of satisfaction as she meticulously runs through her detailed research.

"Interesting. Where will the company be located?"

"In Downtown Detroit."

"How far is that from your respective area?" he asked with grave concern. Knowing that Eight Mile Road was quiet a distance from downtown Detroit.

"It would take them roughly thirty minutes to commute. But here is the beauty of living in my community; we would provide executive *door-to-door* transportation service, for a small fee of course." Her smile lit up the room as she clapped her hands together subtly in much amazement, and then added, "This development is going to be one-of-a-kind."

"How many executives do they have?" he asked as his voice hinted at only a few.

"There are thirty-two if you count the Directors."

"Well, Mrs. Deveraux, you have certainly done your homework," he said with a striking smile.

"And once I get *SoftLine* executives to come aboard, we will have the others beating down the door to compete or partake in the luxuries that their counterparts are experiencing."

"This is a massive project that you have taken on; surely you will seek some sort of bank funding to help finance this deal? I am confident, of course, that you have the means to fund this project on your own but why would you risk your own money," Wesley said, and then continued, "the financial market has taken quite a hit in the past couple of years and we need to hold on to every dollar, if I may add."

Mrs. Deveraux remained silent as if she had to ponder his question but she had suspected this sort of question. She always expected these questions. It was what made her good at what she did—*convincing others to see it her way and anticipating their questions*. But, today, she simply leaned her head back comfortably along the backing of an 18th century custom upholstered wing back chair and softly released a gentle sigh. She took in the faint crackle from the roaring classical fireplace that cast a romantic silhouette like in a 17th century castle. She marveled over the stucco ceilings that mimicked a fascinating French restaurant that she had once visited while in France but suddenly couldn't recall the name. Her thoughts lingered for more than a few minutes.

Wesley watched as her eyelids seem to move in slow motion. Her stretched long slim neck that illuminated the low cut V-neck blouse that she wore which revealed a subtle hint of her voluptuous breast glowed from the illusion of daylight that sprayed through the sheer drapery. She licked her neatly framed lips with a stroke of her tongue, with such delicacy as if she didn't want to frighten them from her face. He watched her elegant demeanor and was mesmerized by her stunning appearance. Beauty and brains...an intriguing but lethal combination for a woman, he thought. His face glimmered with enchanting delight as if he was admiring the four hundred figures of saints, prophets and angles inside the magnificent walls of the *Wells Cathedral* in England.

Fearing that Mrs. Deveraux would bend her head for a short glance at him; he interrupted their comfortable silence. "I believe that commercial real estate was at its most lucrative in the mid 1980's, but by 1987 the real estate market had its share of turmoil. Many experts suspect that this recession will be similar."

"Yes, that was a time of great appreciation and much achievement," she finally spoke and added, "it was a time when homeowners took pride in their homes and credit was easier to come by. It was the imbalance of supply and demand that crumbled the real estate market back then. I have probably thought about this more than you care to know. Real estate isn't going anywhere. No matter what the big wigs in Washington may think or want the people to think."

She raised her head from the backing of the chair and affixed her charismatic eyes on Wesley. "I have been in this business a *very long* time, Mr. Wesley. I can assure you that this project will go through as planned and it will be very lucrative and successful," she said. Her words were crisp, starched and pressed, and then she continued, "There was a time when businesses flourished without the meddling of city officials, codes, and regulations of property lines. Businesses didn't recede because of economic, political, or social circumstances. They flourished from the help and patronage of everyday people. If a business was going under the community would rally together to keep it in business." She released another long steady sigh, resting her head along the backing of the chair again. "Not anymore. I use to be one of those people. I could not be swayed by the amount of money I would make on a deal but rather the excitement from the achievement of a goal. All that has changed," she said in a soft manner.

He felt a chill run up his spin as he listened deeply to her soft-spoken words. A voice he had not heard before. A shuddered voice that captured his soul. Her weeping tone dismissed her *la-di-da* attitude. He thought she would shed a tear but her arrogance wouldn't allow one to fall. He couldn't tell if this was a ploy or sincere words of dismay, but it was intriguing all the same.

"Ok, Mrs. Deveraux, I will consider your request. Let me think about it and have my accountant and the like put some numbers together to see if it would be feasible to establish a mark within your development. I will inform you of my answer before week's end," he earnestly stated.

Chapter 8

The Legal Ramifications of Greed

"YOUR HONOR, THESE PROCEEDINGS HAVE eaten up enough of the tax payer's money, so I move for a motion to dismiss in light of the evidence," Attorney Locklair demanded.

"What evidence?" District Attorney Kevin Marlinton shouted.

"Ok, ok...this has turned into a shouting match. This case has gone on long enough. Frankly, I am tired of hearing it. Both of you have come to my courtroom with the same mediocre evidence which hasn't convinced me one way or the other. You have two weeks to present a worthwhile case to me or I will be forced to throw it out and move you to another judge's courtroom. And you would have to start this charade all over again in another five years.

"Your Honor, there is *no* evidence. The only documents that have been presented in this courtroom are forged—" Marlinton stated.

Locklair interrupted, "—no evidence of forged documents, Your Honor. This is preposterous."

"Gentlemen, I am not going to have this debate again. My decision stands. Two weeks or this case goes out the window," Judge Remington stated.

"Does she have everyone in her back pocket," Marlinton hissed.

"What was that?" Judge Remington demanded.

"I'm sorry Sir...what are you asking?" Marlinton mockingly asked as he began packing up his scattered papers.

"What was the comment you muttered?" he asked impatiently.

"Sir...it seems that every time we bring in evidence or an expert witness to contest what the defense attorney has presented as evidence, it's not enough. An expert witness testified that the signed documents in question could not have been signed by the alleged deceased, Mr. Wendell Grimshaw. We have several other documents that we believe were signed under duress as well. The *Evidence of Title* seems to be missing from Ronald Smits's file in which the defendant admits to visiting Mr. Smits the day he was murdered. We are simply asking for this case to be heard in a courtroom of her peers and let justice prevail," he stated matter-of-factly.

"Well, this *so-called* case has been brought to me to determine if there is enough evidence for it to go to trial. I still feel that you have not stated your case, Mr. Marlinton. The statements that you have mentioned have not been submitted as factual information or events. All you have so far is hearsay and conjectures. The documents presented appeared to be legitimate and your expert could not conclusively determine that Mr. Wendell Grimshaw did not sign the documents.

"Furthermore, most of this so-called evidence is for a civil court, not criminal court. You need to determine what crimes the defendant has committed and prosecute your case accordingly. We hear criminal cases in this courtroom, Mr. Marlinton; the civil courtroom is down the hall. Are you charging the defendant with embezzlement, forgery, and falsifying legal documents or are you charging the defendant with murder? Be that as it may, these are criminal offenses, Mr. Marlinton.

"As for your comment, I am appalled. I stand for *justice* in this courtroom and the mere fact that you have insinuated that I could represent anything other than justice is *preposterous*—as Mr. Locklair has strongly indicated. Now, come to me in two weeks with a *real* case. Stop your whining Mr. Marlinton and do your job.

If you have evidence that is relevant to *this* case, then I would definitely like to hear it."

"She has a court proceeding in Judge Meacham's court over the rights to the Wendell Grimshaw Estate. This case; CASE NO.342-5124 is tied to CASE NO.412-7812 in Judge Meacham's courtroom," Marlinton added.

"*Save it, Mr. Marlinton.* I have heard enough. You need to provide evidence that is relative to *this* case, a criminal case. Please keep that in mind when you submit this evidence to my courtroom in two weeks," Judge Remington forewarned.

"Your Honor, if I may, this case has been going on for over a year now and I don't really see the need to make my client wait another day. My client's properties have been held up in court proceedings for over nine years. This is the last property in question and I don't think that it is fair to penalize my client for the DA's inadequacies."

"Fair statement Mr. Locklair but your client should have made sure that her investments were well protected. I can't say if the documents in question are forged or not but the mere fact that it has reached the DA's office and into my courtroom has to be of great concern to the community that we've sworn to protect,—"

"I understand that Your Honor but my client is a tax paying citizen in the community and the laws are made to protect her interest as well. The documents clearly show the Right to Survivorship clause (as any partnership contract would state) and the Deed of Release from each interested party. We also have bank statements that show money transfers to each partner for their interest in the land or property," Locklair politely interrupted.

"All your documents are false. You have what she made up," Mr. Marlinton sharply stated.

"My client simply covered all the bases…she *was* protecting her interest," Locklair strongly disagreed and offered a disdainful comment of his own.

"My decision stands— two weeks, that's it, counsels.

"Is that bitch ever going to pay for her actions," a voice from the crowd in the courtroom bellowed.

The crowd shuffled around noisily to get a glimpse of the voice while the judge pounds his gavel to maintain order. "Who said that? There will be no outburst in my courtroom. *Order!*" Judge Remington firmly demanded.

An unfamiliar face surfaced from the crowd of spectators. A handsome man. Young. A profound look of intensity covered his face. His dreamy magnetic gray eyes forced their way into your soul and your breath collapsed. The gripping sound of his voice made you shiver. And as he strolled to the front of the mob, which were now standing at this point; his charming charisma smoldered through his skin. At least, that was how Mrs. Deveraux saw it. "Tom," she managed a whisper. A wry smile drifted in place but only for a short moment. She didn't want to give herself away.

"Do you have to have everything? Isn't it bad enough that you took over the entire Grimshaw estate; do you have to have this too? When are you going to end this?" he shouted.

Judge Remington pounds his gavel several more times to hush the crowd. "Sir, I will not tolerate outburst in my courtroom. I will be forced to lock you up for contempt if you do not cease this nonsense immediately," he forewarned.

"Haven't you heard enough of this foolishness to make a ruling? She is lying, can't you see that?" the voice cried out.

Mrs. Deveraux could hear the crack in his voice and she felt the frustration that manifested from his heart. She saw a confused, fatigued, splendidly dressed young man. She thought that perhaps he was Tom but his shifting attitude convinced her that he was simply another member of one of the families that persuaded the DA to take this case to court.

"What is your name, son?" Judge Remington asked with a hint of irritation.

"Garraty...Anthony Garraty," the voice answered.

"Mr. Garraty, what is your interest in this case?" Judge Remington asked.

The crowd moved about in a nearly silent manner awaiting Garraty's response.

"I'm Heather Smits's husband. One of the deceased, Ronald Smits, Heather is his youngest daughter," he stated.

"So, are you saying that you are the son-in-law of one of the property owners?" Judge Remington asked.

"Yes."

"Well, I do understand your grief but we have rules in this courtroom and I don't like outburst, they are very disruptive. If you have evidence that pertains to this case, then you should forward that information to the District Attorney."

"I understand that Sir, but she has been in this courtroom more than anyone cares to count and yet she is still given the benefit-of-the-doubt. It seems that the law has always moved in her favor."

"Mr. Garraty, the DA has to prove that the defendant has broken a law. The burden of proof is on the prosecutor, not the defendant. Now, if you have information that would assist the prosecutor in making his case, I strongly suggest that you provide that to Mr. Marlinton. But for now, I must ask you again to control yourself for the remainder of these proceedings or I will be forced to have you removed from my courtroom," Judge Remington firmly stated.

"This isn't the end, Mrs. Deveraux. You have stepped on one too many people. Your end is nearing." he hissed, looking Mrs. Deveraux directly in the eyes.

"Are you threatening me Mr. Garraty?" she asked.

"What…are you going to kill me like you did Ronald Smits?"

"This man is out of control, Your Honor." Locklair shouted.

"Mr. Garraty, you are pushing your luck…please, have a seat and keep quiet," Judge Remington stated.

Mr. Garraty turned his back and headed for the exit doors. He stopped to glance over his shoulder and blurted, "You will pay for what you have done to my family, Mrs. Deveraux. You can bet your sweet ass on that."

The spectators that milled about in the courtroom, eyes filled with astonishment, had shifted their bodies to make way for Mr. Garraty. The lawyers were baffled beyond belief and the judge hammered his gavel for order. No one had ever threatened a defendant in open court before, at least not in this town and especially not this defendant. They were stunned as to what should be done. "Mr. Garraty is now in contempt. Grab him before he leaves the courtroom," Judge Remington ordered.

Garraty made a dash for the door but the heavy bailiff was much faster than he appeared. He raced to the back of the courtroom, leaped over a few bench seats and landed on Garraty, throwing his body weight on top of Garraty to wrestle him to the floor. The bailiff moved so swiftly that by the time he stood up from the floor, he had Mr. Garraty in handcuffs and facing the judge.

mrs. deveraux

"Book 'em," Judge Remington said solemnly.

Chapter 9

A Degree in Murder

AS RAZOR SHARP AS BRIDGES' MIND, SHE HAD overlooked the subtle consistencies with each crime scene. However, it didn't take her long to uncover the mysteries of these cases. She placed a piece of loose-leaf paper on top of her hollow metal desk that sat in a back corner in the police station. She had first been offended by the backseat but after a while she had grown accustomed to it. It had been her thinking tunnel; her moment of salvation. Her desk sat several feet from the others behind an empty desk that was filling rapidly with boxes of case files that had been neglected due to the overwhelming demand of the town's first serial killer case.

She opened the files: SMITS, RONALD AND DEBRA and LANGDON III, OXFORD AND SAMANTHA. She glanced over the Smits file first, scattering the file's contents across the desk: the crime scene photos, the police report, and the medical examiner's report. Then she glanced at the Langdon file.

Nothing.

She knew she was missing something. So far, it appeared that they had three homicides that were committed by the same killer and now a fourth.

She read the police report for the Smits murders, the first victims. "I know the answer lies within this first killing...I'm sure of it," she mumbled to herself.

The deceased is an adult white male found in a semi-prone position with his arms and legs severed from his torso...arms are vertically positioned next to the body with the left hand nailed to the hardwood floor...the left side of his face was in contact with the floor while the right side remained visible. There is a single gunshot wound to the head – in the middle of the forehead...a large bloodstain (a pool of blood) surrounds his head...brain matter...bone fragments...and blood running from the nose across his lips and passing down his cheeks to the floor...

The deceased...adult white female was found in the master bathroom, kneeling on her knees with her bottom in the air leaning against the bath tub with the weight of her body resting on the outer side of each forearm. The bottom of her right foot was visible and the left foot lay partially flat on the travertine floor...the right foot appears to have dirt smeared on the bottom of the entire foot...soil seems fresh...

"The husband appears to have been crucified like Jesus and the wife was kneeling in prayer," Bridges whispered to herself. "This has got to mean something...but what?"

She opened a yellow envelop and pulled out the crime scene photos from the Smits murder: several dozens of sharp color photos blown up to 8 ½" x 10". "What am I missing here," she whispered. Staring intensely at the photo of Mrs. Smits lying on the bathroom floor, "It has got to be in one of these photos."

Her eyes steadily moved across the other photos and soon she fixed her eyes on the wall behind the Smits's desk. She leaned forward, moving her head closer to the desk. She lifted the photo with her left hand and faintly brushed it with her right, as if she were clearing the dust from an old childhood picture. *"What type of painting is that?"* she said aloud. She eagerly moved her eyes across the photo and noticed the unusual tilted painting that clung to life behind the executive office chair. It appeared quite amateurish but may have been painted by a professional, Bridges thought.

While attending Cambridge, she studied art pieces as a hobby to keep her mind off home. Of course, she was a dilettante of art herself. Bridges was at the beginning stages of distinguishing professional art from the art that parents adore. "It appears to be incomplete," she thought to herself.

"That's it…it's gotta be it," she said with excitement as if she had cracked the case. But in the back of her mind she didn't know what this painting meant, if anything. It just simply appeared out of place from the rest of the décor.

Although the painting seemed recreational, it did have a distinguished look of an expensive piece. "It must be the type of painting that…I need to go back to the Smits home and collect that painting." Her eyes gazed into the air for a fleeting moment, and then she opened the Langdon file again. She pulled out the photos and immediately scanned through them to find the pictures from Mr. Langdon's study. She searched the photos but the crime scene techs didn't capture many photos of Mr. Langdon's office wall. "Dammit," she barked.

She tossed the photos on the desk, leaned back in her squeaky chair, and rested her interlocked hands along the back of her neck. She inspected the photos in front of her and one stood out. She thrust forward, nearly bouncing from her chair, and snatched up a photo that was partially hiding underneath another. She noticed a small painting tucked underneath a stack of scattered papers. From what Bridges could see, it appeared to be the same bold and vivid colors that were in the painting at the Smits's mansion.

There were almost a dozen pictures of the desk alone, presumably because the killer had left the Smits crime scene neat and orderly. Then Bridges remembered Det. Jarrod had indicated that Mr. Langdon was not a meticulous organized man as Mr. Smits. "Ok, I know I'm not trippin'. There has got to be something about these darn paintings," she said aloud. "I better start writing this down. I need to revisit both crime scenes."

She grabbed a pen from an inadequate pencil holder used to shelter a collection of ink pens that seldom worked. *Allure 'de Champaign* was carved into the high-quality porcelain cup. She had not noticed its unique elegant look before. She studied the cup for what seemed like an hour before she realized that she had drifted under like a spell. She jerked her head, bucked her eyes, raised her brow, and wondered why she suddenly became consumed with this original cup. "That's it dammit," she whispered. Pounding the desk with an enclosed fist, hopped from her chair, and rushed to the Captain's office.

He was gone.

"Damn. I need to get access to Mrs. Deveraux's old case files," she said aloud. "I'm sure the Captain would never allow this but at least I'm not insisting on questioning her, whom I believe should be questioned," she whispered to herself again.

She stared at the Captain's chair with such intense as if he would magically appear. She snapped out of her daze and paced herself back to her desk.

"I can go to the county courthouse. They have got to have a record of all her court cases. They must." she muttered with enthusiasm while on the way back to her desk. "These homicide cases are somehow tied to Mrs. Deveraux, I'm sure of it. There has got to be a connection. She is trying to close the deal of a life time and these prominent deceased real estate developers didn't want to play ball.

"But if this is true…why are these murders so brutal and violent? Do these paintings have any significance? If so, what?" She pondered for a minute and muttered, "I'll start with the case files in our station records."

She made it back to her desk, focused on the blank sheet of paper and started writing.

alina

THE CRIME SCENE of the second set of victims was just as horrendous and thespian as the first. Oxford and Samantha Langdon III had started their day like any other. Oxford had prepared for his morning meeting with a prospective client and Samantha headed out the door at seven fifteen a.m. on her way to the office.

Samantha worked as a volunteer for a small publishing company. She had been working there over twelve years and at age sixty-seven, she wasn't handsomely seeking retirement. She took pride in being a part of something mystical, as she would put it. She thought that writers were so mysterious and clever. "How do they come up with such story lines," she would say.

But nothing was as mystical and mysterious as her husband. A barrel-chested man; stylish neatly tapered salt & pepper hair; a firm but astonishingly soothing deep voice; and a provocative smile that would steel any woman's heart and leave her breathless.

Even as he lay on the floor of their master bedroom, silenced by a single bullet through the middle section of his forehead, his face held a remarkably subtle and calm expression. His ocean blue eyes pierced through your heart like a dagger. Bridges found herself gasping for Mr. Langdon's last breath. She released a deeply held sigh and noticed the stubbles of hair on his cheek. She was aware that it did not take long for men to develop a five-o'clock shadow but the hair along his cheeks seemed to be more than a single night. But she brushed it off and pressed on, not thinking to make a mental note of her observation.

It had become obvious to Det. Bridges that the department had two related murder scenes. She immediately felt that there was a serial killer in the mix.

Reflecting on the crime scene at the Langdon's house, she remembered seeing Sgt. Willowbee. She merely saw a glimpse of his face as she proceeded at a glacial pace to the master bathroom where Mrs. Langdon laid dead from a single shot to the temple. She had briefly considered the thought (of Sgt. Willowbee's presence at their crime scene) but focused her much needed attention on Mrs. Langdon.

As she sat at her metal desk at the station, her mind started to race back in time as if she had tumbled down a steep icy gully. She eagerly tried to place herself back at the scene of the Langdon's house when her eyes had first met Sgt. Willowbee's.

After analyzing the master bathroom, Bridges bolted from the master bedroom to get an intimate view of what Sgt. Willowbee was doing at their crime scene. It really wasn't that unusual to have a Sergeant at the scene of a double homicide and especially a homicide that had all the innerworkings of a serial killer. Except Bridges felt there was something peculiar about Sgt. Willowbee's presence. She had a gut feeling and her instincts were usually right. Furthermore, Captain Crawford had assigned the case to Detective Louise Popper and Det. Bridges. Yet, after they soon determined that the Smits's and the Langdon's murders were related, Captain Crawford wanted a two-man team focused on a specific crime scene.

What once had escaped her mind was now clearly in focus—she could picture an intrusive Sgt. Willowbee shifting the papers that were maddeningly scattered across Mr. Langdon's desk. She recalled that his demeanor didn't read *detective* but *personal*. She concluded that he must have been searching for something, but what, she pondered.

"HEY, WHAT YOU got there," another detective asked, prompting a twitch in Bridges' body causing her to shiver and shriek.

"Don't do that Popper," Bridges' said releasing a startled breath.

"Sorry. Didn't mean to frighten you. What's with the notes?"

"Let me ask you something—"

"—Ok."

"Do you remember seeing Sgt. Willowbee at the Langdon house?"

"Umm…no…wait, yeah, I do remember him being there, why?" she said hesitantly.

"Did you notice anything out of the ordinary about him?"

"You're treading on thin ice Det. Bridges. You don't want to challenge that idea until you can furnish a mountain of proof."

"But I haven't accused him of anything yet. There's nothing to prove; I'm just asking a question," she said with a puzzled expression.

"I recognized the look," Det. Popper stated sarcastically.

Bridges picked up her piece of paper with sedulous care, rested her back to the base of her desk chair and gradually rocked as the chair squeaked and she scanned her handwritten notes. "See, I've been going over the crime scenes in my head—"

"Sometimes you really need to stay out of your head," Popper stated with modest laughter.

"No…I'm serious. I've been playing the Langdon house over and over in my mind trying to determine why Sgt. Willowbee was at our crime scene. He had made it on the scene just as we did or perhaps a little before. Now…it is possible that he may have wanted to see if the Smits's murder was related to the Langdon's murder. However, how would he have known what type of murder it was until he was on the scene or until he read one of our reports? When the call came in to dispatch, the caller stated that she had found the bodies of two people—"

Reaching for her black notepad, "—It was the housekeeper. She wasn't the usual house cleaning lady. It was her first time in the Langdon house and she did not know them by name. Plus, she was an immigrant who didn't speak fluent English. The dispatcher thought she stated that there were two sick buddies so we did not know *exactly* what we were being dispatched for—"

"Following you so far but what's your point." Popper said impatiently.

"Really, I'm trying to get a question answered," she said with a hint of irritation.

"What question?"

"What was Sgt. Willowbee doing at our crime scene? And, what was he searching for at the scene?"

"Searching for—," Popper softly said with a suspicious brow.

"Yes. I distinctly recall him rambling on the Langdon's desk as if he was searching for something and it wasn't evidence."

"That's pretty presumptuous of you Det. Bridges because he could have been surveying the area for potential evidence. He is a veteran you know. They have different ways of solving cases."

"But there was something uniquely different about his browse. He appeared to be looking for something of high importance and of a personal nature—something that he did *not* want the rest of us to see," she boasted confidently.

"You sound so sure of yourself. I still say that you are skating on *very* thin ice and you better go slowly or you will find yourself in a river of bone-chilling water."

"Why is everyone telling me to walk on *eggshells* around Sgt. Willowbee and Mrs. Deveraux? What is the connection with those two?" Bridges said holding a vulgar facial expression.

"Maybe there is *no* connection. Maybe you have given this more consideration than it ought to have. Maybe—"

"Maybe, I'm done with this conversation." Bridges jumped from her chair and headed toward the lobby door.

"I think you may be in over your head Det. Bridges. Proof is what you'll need. Everything else is circumstantial, *without merit*," Popper shouted as Bridges departed the station.

Chapter 10

An Intriguing and Captivating Psychopath

M RS. DEVERAUX'S PAST COURT PROCEEDINGS were exceptionally interesting, Bridges thought. It painted a picture of a greedy, rich, and very powerful woman who would stop at nothing to get what she wanted. But there were some elements of Mrs. Deveraux's background that Bridges found intriguing.

The anonymous documents Bridges received quilted the study table in the station archived records section. There was no forwarding address. No stamp or printed metered *first-class mail* postage affixed in the top right corner of the big yellow envelope to indicate that it had been mailed. Just the information of the intended recipient:

Bloomfield Hills Police Department
Attn: Detective Margret Bridges
5551 W. Boubean Street
Bloomfield Hills, MI 48302

Bridges didn't know what to think of the mysterious package at first; but after she briefly scanned the contents, it was clear she had an ally. There was something bigger at large here and Bridges didn't mean the killer. Someone else was working an angle, but Bridges would take all the help she could get for now. She figured she would investigate the anonymous sender of the package later.

Bridges circled back through the documents from the anonymous sender, re-examined the case files from the station archive records and started at the beginning.

It was rumored that Mrs. Deveraux killed her way into wealth. Of course, the rumors were just as incidental as the copies of suspicious court cases Bridges held in her hand. After an extensive investigation, Bridges was astounded by what she'd discovered.

It seemed that Mrs. Deveraux had a pertinacious need to dominate a situation and ensure that the results were in favor of her mission. Her infectious finesse, unyielding persona and dominating piercing eyes that entrapped you, was how Mrs. Deveraux claimed her victims. It also seemed that Mrs. Deveraux had a talent for engendering and manipulating criminals to do her bidding.

Bridges found Mrs. Deveraux to be nefarious but charming and unforgettable. Bridges thought perhaps it was this charisma that made the boys at the station swoon into believing that Mrs. Deveraux was innocent. Bridges mulled over this thought for a brief moment and dismissed it as quick as it came. She knew Captain Crawford better than that; he is an upstanding cop who would arrest his own brother if he broke the law.

As Bridges methodically examined Mrs. Deveraux's court cases and the information she had obtained during her investigation into Mrs. Deveraux, it became more evident to Bridges that Mrs. Deveraux could very well be the sadistic killer they had been searching for.

BORN IN LONDON, unverifiable information surfaced that Judith Ann Deveraux could have been an ill-legitimate daughter of the Duke of Westminster. Although Mrs. Deveraux's richest couldn't be traced to a particular origin. One thing was for certain, the Duke of Westminster wasn't her father. Mrs. Deveraux's father had been suspected of killing her mother.

It was reported that Mrs. Deveraux returned home one brutally cold afternoon and found her mother butchered. Her mother's raped, beaten, and mutilated body was found stretched across the bed. Her nude body was pallid and bluish. The aroma of decomposition had not yet mystified the air because of the abnormally chilly temperatures. But viewing her mother's gruesome body in such an undermined state was enough to render Mrs. Deveraux aloof. The authorities reported Mrs. Deveraux saying, "It was so much blood…I don't…it was so much blood. Why did they have to do that?"

Mrs. Deveraux was seventeen when her mother was killed and this was most likely her first taste of "real" blood, Bridges thought. Bridges considered how devastating and mind-changing that incident had to be for Mrs. Deveraux. She reviewed the case file and notes further and determined that Mrs. Deveraux's father had been a suspect in her mother's murder.

Mrs. Deveraux's startling story intensified and Bridges found herself purely engulfed in the pages of this unreal tale. She gently collapsed her body against the wall next to the archive section in the basement where they kept most of the department's case files. Filled with sudden anticipation, Bridges turned the pages incessantly waiting for the floor to drop beneath her. She held her breath but hadn't realized it until she exhaled noisily. Jitters exploded inside her like firecrackers. And with every passing word, her eyes bulged more and more. She had been consumed.

After Mrs. Deveraux's mother was butchered, Mrs. Deveraux learned that her father had been the *prime* suspect and *all* other suspects had been detained and released. A few months later the authorities found Mrs. Deveraux's father dead. He had been tortured, beaten beyond detection, and practically beheaded. He had to be identified by his dental records and even that was challenging, noted by the medical examiner.

Mrs. Deveraux was never a suspect. No one would have ever thought that a seventeen-year-old girl would be capable of such a horrendous crime. Furthermore, she was still suffering from the shock of seeing her mother in such a horrific state, one detective indicated. Although there was one cop on the force that insisted it was something about Mrs. Deveraux that made him give her a second look. "There was something in her eyes that I had seen before. It was controlling and possessive. Evil had begun to transform into a new face." Of course, he couldn't prove any of his accusations and they were discharged before they could be of merit; but that cop said he saw blood in her eyes.

Bridges thought, *that cop may have been right*. There was something about her eyes. They were fiercely captivating and compelling to some and evil and relentless to others; yet, somehow, her breathtaking beauty poured through you like rain manipulating your judgement. It was a strange passive thought and Bridges couldn't understand why she had been engrossed with such a thought.

"I can't be having these strange conflicting emotions about this woman, she's a murderer," Bridges mumbled to herself and kept reading.

Bridges learned that Mrs. Deveraux was accused of money laundering when she moved from New York to Michigan. It was suspected that she laundered money for organized crime members through her real estate transactions. Her husband, Mr. Deveraux had been the primary focus of the police's investigation. As if Mrs. Deveraux's power couldn't get any stranger, Bridges also learned that Mr. Deveraux's last name was not *Deveraux* at all. His last name was *Wilson*. And after the police couldn't arrest Mr. Deveraux for the crimes he was accused; he and Mrs. Deveraux were married and no law enforcement officer had ever pursued the money laundering matter again.

"Wilson? What is going on here? Who takes the name of their *wife*?" Bridges said excitingly and whispered further, "a guilty man, that's who."

Bridges poured through the case files, coming across Case No. 32416-200. The enthusiasm had overwhelmed her and with a brow raised and much intensity, she continued reading. Each page competing for her attention. Bridges brow furrowed when she read how the police brought Mrs. Deveraux in for questioning, and she took the entire police department to court for harassment, planting evidence, and falsifying police reports. It was a mess. Mrs. Deveraux's accusations launched an extensive Internal Affairs investigation against Sgt. Willowbee, Captain Crawford, and several other officers who were fired for corrupt behavior and some were eventually forced to retire. After the Internal Affairs investigation, which was handed down by the Governor of course, the Bloomfield Hills Police Department was forced to drop the charges against Mrs. Deveraux and reflectively, she was forced to drop the lawsuit.

"This has got to be why Sgt. Willowbee and the Captain don't want to question Mrs. Deveraux," she said colorfully but with a hardened face. "But why was Sgt. Willowbee acting so weird? He's too close to retirement and he may be trying to cut a deal with the Devil to ensure a handsome retirement fund." She paused for a moment, blurred out the writing on the pages before her and unknowingly emptied her mind.

After several unimpaired minutes, Bridges' confusion resurfaced, "I don't know. I don't think…maybe…I have to be sure to cover all angles," she thought mercifully.

As Bridges continued to scan through the remaining documents, the Wendell Grimshaw Estate case brought her scanning to a halt. She read the court transcripts audibly and in a faint whisper. Any doubtful thoughts Bridges had about Mrs. Deveraux's power was emphatically changed after reading how Mrs. Deveraux calculatingly took over an entire estate with the whole world watching. "This woman is something else…" Her eyes moved across the pages with such speed Bridges thought she felt a swift breeze of wind move across the tip of her nose. She softly swept her right index finger across her nose, eyes never leaving the transcripts and continued reading.

"Why don't she just brand her initials on the chest of everyone she has ever screwed, *property of Mrs. D.*

"What judge allowed this to happen? I can't believe no one stepped forward to claim the Grimshaw Family inheritance…there had to be at least one family member left," Bridges thought while loosely dropping her arms in dismay. She gazed straight ahead and her mind was suddenly infused with sophomoric notions. Bridges wanted to kick the life out of the seasoned veterans that couldn't see *right* through Mrs. Deveraux's deceitful web. "I guess her erotic persuasion convinced the powers that be to grant such as request. They ate her nonsense up like candy. How remarkable…this woman." Bridges uttered with an uncanny leer.

Bridges mission now was to find an heir to the Wendell Grimshaw Estate, "There has got to be someone left, perhaps a niece or nephew or grandchild…*someone.*"

Chapter 11

A Blackmailer Named Tom

"I FOLLOWED YOUR DAY IN COURT, JULIE ANN," the caller stated.

"Who is this? Is that you again Tom?" Mrs. Deveraux asked.

"I'm touched, you remembered my voice. Are you still trying to analyze me Julie Ann?"

She faintly laughed, "So, what do I owe the pleasure of this phone call?"

"I want to let bygones be bygones. We got off to a rough start and I would like to apologize for not meeting you at the property in question."

"What can I do for you Mr. Tom?" she said exhaustingly.

"Oh, I see, you want to get right down to business. This time, we'll do it your way. Here's the deal: Stop your project…*immediately.*"

"Or what," she hissed. Not feeling in the mood to play games on this day, Mrs. Deveraux didn't wait for a response from Tom, she simply pressed end on her cell phone.

When her phone rang again, she ignored it. After three failed attempts, she finally picked up the phone and pressed the green phone on the screen to accept the call. Before she could say hello, Tom abruptly shouted, "I'm not playing with you lady."

"Tom," Mrs. Deveraux calmly whispered, showing little concern and then she continued, "I don't want to play games today. So, I am ending this conversation before it begins."

Tom tried so desperately to conceal his frustration. He offhandedly tried to clear the knot forming inside his throat but his attempts didn't elude Mrs. Deveraux. She inadvertently smiled and a feeling of cynicism whiffed across her face.

"Oh, Tom, at times we have to do what we must; and this is one of those times that I must interrupt this boyish act of yours and demand we speak at a later date."

You could feel the steam seeping from Tom's head. Unabashed, he said, "I don't think you realize who you are dealing with Mrs. Deveraux."

"So, we are back to *Mrs. Deveraux*, what happened to *Julie Ann*?"

"Don't be a pompous asshole lady; you don't get to run the show anymore."

"You sound upset Tom. I can't fathom why you would be so upset. Is it because I don't feel the need to play your little game today," she stated in a condescending but pleasant sensuous voice that softened a man's soul. "Aww Tom, don't be upset. It doesn't suit you. Just when we were beginning to have such fun.

"You know, I admired your tenacity and your uncanny persona. I thought I had met my match, and I must admit that I was taken back a little by your unyielding tongue."

Mrs. Deveraux paused for a brief second, and then continued her mockery.

"Perhaps those words and threats you expressed was just that, *words and threats*. Well, Mr. Tom, I'm not one to make threats, I only make promises and I always keep my promises."

Tom had been enthralled and entangled inside the web of Mrs. Deveraux's provocative voice. He had dismissed his frustrations and a pleasurable feeling took over him. He was clearly trapped in a spell of serpent limbs that he couldn't escape. Her insufferable attitude and astonishing effect on people's emotions was overwhelmingly intriguing, he finally managed a thought. *"You are one cold-hearted bitch."*

"Let's not be so harsh, Mr. Tom. Let's try another word, shall we." She laughed feebly and hung up the phone. She wouldn't answer any more of Tom's calls for the rest of the night.

Mrs. Deveraux continued to mingle with her guest as she hosted another one of her famous charity events in downtown Detroit. The champagne filled flutes were passed around by the waiters; the personalized chef created food was being inhaled and at ten thousand per plate, it had better be worth it. Of course, the food was much to be desired but even after a three-course meal, most of the guest's stomachs were not fulfilled. But charity events were about the money and these billionaires had lots of it.

Mrs. Deveraux had been consumed with her phone conversation with Tom, she hadn't noticed her food. She smiled and meticulously rubbed her fingers around the rim of her champagne glass, contemplating her next move. She seemed oddly disappointed in Tom. She thought he was a challenge for her. She thought she would have a little fun with him. Then she gazed at her glass of champagne and an eerie feeling chilled her. She shuddered. "I can't underestimate this guy. I have got to find out who he is and what he truly wants. Why would he want me to stop my projects? How does he even know about my projects? I have got to get answers. This is *unacceptable*," she muttered to herself as she intentionally tuned out the guest speaker who stood at the podium talking about nothing. "Just hand over the check is what he really wants to say, I'm sure," she blurted aloud, but her sudden broadcast went unnoticed.

MRS. DEVERAUX DECIDED to hire a private investigator to check into her dear friend Tom. She had to know what he was up to and why he seemed so concerned with her affairs. Of course, everyone these days were overly concerned with my affairs, she thought. "I have got to get to the bottom of this and put an end to this travesty. If I must start eliminating people, then that is what I must do."

"Mrs. Deveraux, who must you eliminate?"

"I'm just rambling dear, no worries. I do need you to find out who Tom is though. I need to know what his interest is in my building." For a moment, it escaped her mind that she was on the phone with Mr. Mullens.

"Not a problem, Mrs. Deveraux. I will find out who he is and what he wants. From what you were telling me earlier, he doesn't sound like a person that will give up easily, so this could get pretty hairy," Jim Mullens alleged. Jim is a retired CIA agent turned private investigator. Of course, no one really knows about his

CIA days except Mrs. Deveraux. If anyone can uncover the mystery of Tom, Jim can.

"I know Jim, but I trust you will be able to get to the bottom of things."

"And you know that I will. Don't worry, I will take care of it."

"I'm not worried."

And with no notice, just as she had done before, she hung up. *Click.*

Mrs. Deveraux was accustomed to handling sticky situations on her own and although she had faith in Mr. Mullens, she still felt compelled to conduct her own research. In the back of her mind she knew there was a deep dark unpleasant side to what was about to come. For the remainder of the day, Mrs. Deveraux's mind became consumed with finding out the truth to this interminable saga. In spite all her gratifying moments of control, Mrs. Deveraux had never felt she was losing control, until today.

"I can't remember the last time I took a Valium. Well, nevertheless, it will help calm me and perhaps I could try and get some sleep," Mrs. Deveraux said to herself as she mingled about, moving from the living room to the bathroom, to the bedroom. "I don't know why I am so worked up anyway." She crawled into bed, ignoring the flashing message light on her landline phone which indicated that she had a message and closed her eyes to sleep.

alina

THE DARKNESS HAD swallowed up the bedroom as Mrs. Deveraux fell fast asleep. Her dreams were unhurried and her mind had just begun to clear, and then suddenly, a loud thump had awakened her. Still in a stage of disorientation from the Valium, she rolled over to her right side and slowly opened her weak eyelids.

Nothing was there.

"Hello," she muttered in a faded voice. She tried to sit up but her relaxed state made it challenging so she simply rolled on her back, took in a soft quaint sigh, and exhaled, "hello, is that you Clayton?"

No response.

She closed her eyelids and rested her head on her pillow for a short-lived moment before a dark shadow quickly wafts by the end of Mrs. Deveraux's bed. She could feel an intensity rush through her body. She frightfully, but slowly maneuvered her head back and forth, side to side, without lifting her head from the pillow. She felt a warm figure move closer to her. In an instant, a hint of hot breath whistled across her delicate face. Her eyelids remained closed as a tingle of fear discharged through her body. She felt a sickening pressure take hold of her lungs. Her muscles moved anxiously inside her body but were unseen outside the walls of her skin. Her blanched skin reeked of a slow death. It seemed the life was being sucked out of her. She knew she was dying.

For once, she couldn't move…she couldn't speak…she couldn't think.

"Julie Ann," she heard her name soar weightless through the air in a song. "Julie Ann," there it goes again. Her eyes moved under her closed eyelids and the fright tortured her senses. This very moment inflated her mind with monstrous illusions. As the venom of fear pumped through her veins she could envision the dark shadow covering her mouth with old used rags. She submerged her face inside the rags and waited for her breath to stop. She waited for her heart to skip a beat. She waited for the inexorable moment when her brain would flounder. In this sudden wake of terror, she felt powerless.

"Julie Ann," the song rang out again.

She moved her head from side to side in a quicker motion than before. She tried opening her eyes but they felt heavy. She tried moving her hands, and then her arms but it was useless. Her limbs felt pinned down to the bed. Horrific thoughts tunneled throughout her mind as she envisioned the bodies of Ronald Smits and Jim Holmes. She could clearly see their severed legs walking across her bedroom floor. Her brain gnawed on the idea of the severed legs attacking her as they moved in closer to her bed. She visualized their wives' big blank black eyeballs staring at her, mutely declaring an answer to an unknown question. "What is the question," her brain finally captured a thought.

"You know the question Julie Ann. *Why*?"

"*Why what…what…what do you want from me?*"

"I want you Julie Ann. I want you to suffer just as I have. It's the end of the road for you Julie Ann. It's the…"

Before the whisper could conclude, Mrs. Deveraux forced opened her eyes and like magic, the dark shadow was gone. She glanced around the room, heavy breath, and scarce judgment. The sensation she felt was both provocative and violent. The passionate hold that lingered over her bosom, pinning down her arms, was a powerful force to be reckoned with. She didn't know what to think of that intensified episode. With trembling hands, she gradually wiped the perspiration off her forehead and stared at her hand, mortified by what she saw. "I'm sweating. *What is happening to me?* I just had a nightmare over this…this…whatever this is. What is coming over me?"

She laid her head on the pillow in dismay and looked straight ahead and spoke distinctly, "I have got to get a hold of this situation. This situation with Tom has affected by bearings and it must cease at once."

Without knowing, Mrs. Deveraux just had an intimate struggle with the Devil, and she skeptically embraced the fact that she still needed to answer the question of *why*. This dream was merely a wake-up call for Mrs. Deveraux and she felt determined to find out *why* Tom was coming after her and what could he possibly know. Being dissatisfied with the wretched thoughts pondering in her mind, she realized that the only way she could stop these disillusions was to confront her ghost and put a knife through his heart.

Her mission became apparent and she knew what she needed to do.

Chapter 12

Follow the Clues

"CAPTAIN, I THINK WE MAY HAVE FOUND A connection with the Vics," Det. Jarrod stated with much enthusiasm.

"Ok, what've you got?" Captain Crawford asked as he crossed his arms against his chest, leaned back in his office chair, and narrowed his eyes sharply waiting impatiently for Det. Jarrod to continue.

"Well, I may have found a connection with most of the Vics," Det. Jarrod stood corrected.

"Ok—"

"They were all very rich high powered real estate developers and all of our Vics except for the Palowski's had an interest in the rundown building and land on Detroit's Westside."

"Interesting. And what else do you have?"

"If the killer's interest is in the building and land, then he may be killing everyone tied to that property. If that is the case, I may know who his next target will be," Det. Jarrod exclaimed.

"Go on," Captain Crawford said uneasily.

"I believe the next victim may be Mrs. Deveraux," Det. Jarrod said cautiously.

"You gotta be kidding me."

"No Sir, I think she may have been the primary target and for reasons unknown at this time, the killer chose to kill her partners instead of her. I think he may be saving her for last."

"Come on Jarrod. There has got to be something else. Another reason or something," Captain Crawford declared and moved in close to Det. Jarrod and lowered his voice, "are you sure this is the way to go 'cause I don't want this getting out and it turns out to be dog shit."

"Sir, I have played this over and over in my head and this certainly has something to do with Mrs. Deveraux. I have asked myself is she a victim or a killer. She has great interest in the land and property in question but is she willing to kill for it? I know she is cold-hearted but I don't think she is a mutilating psychopath."

"I would have to agree. Ok, we have to tread lightly on this. God knows we don't want the wrong ideas getting into the limelight. We will keep this between you and me for now, ok."

"You got it Sir. I will look into this property deal to find all the players and see if I can link any others to this deal that may have mystified us. There has to be someone that we don't have on our radar…like, *the killer*, for instance."

They both smiled and Captain Crawford pats Det. Jarrod on the back, insinuating, *good job* and added, "Not a word, Det. Jarrod. Not a word until we can wrap our heads around this."

Det. Jarrod nods his head in an amendable gesture as he opened the door to walk out of the Captain's office.

Looking back at the Captain, Det. Jarrod turned sharply to exit the office and collided with Det. Bridges.

"Oh, sorry, I'm sorry Det. Jarrod. I thought you saw me," Det. Bridges stated as she tried to catch her sudden breath loss.

Det. Jarrod was equally stunned, and responded, "It's cool Bridges. I should've been watching. Well, he's all yours."

"Actually, I wanted to talk to you first."

"Me? Ok, what's up?"

"Hey, Captain, I will be back to speak with you too," Bridges shouted as her and Det. Jarrod walked away from Captain Crawford's office.

"I'm sure you will Bridges. I'm sure you will," Captain Crawford shouted back with much exasperation. "I'm sure you will and discuss Mrs. Deveraux no doubt," he added in a whisper that only he could hear.

"Here's what I've got. Well, I really have a question for you."

"Ok, shoot," Det. Jarrod said.

"Have you noticed Sgt. Willowbee's behavior lately?" Bridges whispered.

"What do you mean?"

"Well, I'm not accusing him of anything…" Bridges paused, searched the room and continued, "I'm not sure, but I think he may be up to something."

"He's supposed to be up to something. Hell, all of us are up to something, we better be because we have a diabolical psychopath on our hands and no one knows his face," Det. Jarrod proclaimed.

"No. I mean he was at our crime scene the other day and something didn't feel right with his browse."

"He was at your crime scene…the Langdon murders?"

"Yes, and it didn't seem routine to me. I may be way off base but something isn't right," Bridges stated with frozen eyes, fixated on Det. Jarrod's demeanor.

"What do you mean it didn't seem routine to you? Nothing in this case rings routine."

"I know that, but have you noticed any strange or out-of-the ordinary behavior—"

"*Wait a minute,*" Det. Jarrod said excitingly, interrupting Bridges statement.

"What...what is it?"

"He was at my crime scene too. I didn't think anything of it at first but later it brushed across my mind but I dismissed it. He was browsing around at the Holmes estate." Det. Jarrod's eyes stared off into space. He shook his head to release his mind from the trance and then added, "Naw, we must be way off course. We've got to be. I mean, he's a respected officer of the law and I don't think he would bend it for anyone."

"I don't know Jarrod. But what if he was backed into a corner, what then? When a man is close to retirement and desperate, he may do just about anything," Bridges said surely.

"Who said he's desperate? I don't think so Bridges. What've you got to back this theory up aside from the fact that his browse seemed questionable or strange or even perhaps out of the ordinary. What have you got?" he said defensively.

"Well, nothing definitive yet but I know there is more to his story."

"There is more to all of our stories, Bridges. Just because the man's behavior seemed a little odd doesn't mean that he's up to no good."

"So what's your story?" Bridges asked sarcastically.

Det. Jarrod laughed and said, "My story…it's not that interesting."

"Avoiding the question…"

"I tell you what, I don't think we need to worry about Sgt. Willowbee but you bring me something more concrete and I will back you on this. But it has got to be rock solid, I don't want to be scratching my balls from the inside of a jail cell."

"Ok, you got it. If there is something corrupt here, you know my nosy ass will get to the bottom of it." She laughed and walked away.

"Remember Bridges, concrete," Det. Jarrod shouts as Bridges leaves the station.

BRIDGES ABRUPTLY ANSWERED her cell phone, "Hello."

"I'm sorry, did I catch you at a bad time?"

"No, no, Dr. Burke. Please forgive me, I have a lot running through my head right now. What've you got?"

"Trust me, I understand. I may have some information that will be beneficial to your investigation. I'm sure you could use a lifeline," Dr. Burke proclaimed wryly.

alina

Bridges smirked and confirmed, "Yes, we can Dr. Burke. We need all the help we can get. What've you got for me?"

"I examined the blood work and bone fragments you sent to my lab and it appears that Oxford Langdon was killed around four and seven p.m. However, his wife, Mrs. Langdon time of death was around five and seven a.m.," Dr. Burke said with excitement.

"That confirms what the M.E. reported. The lingering question is why there was seemingly fresh blood next to Mr. Langdon's body," Bridges asked.

"The fresh blood wasn't his."

"What? What do you mean? Whose blood was it?"

A heart-wrenching silence penetrated through the phone.

"Was it the killer's blood, please tell me it was the killer's blood." Bridges coarsened voice became ragged and immersed.

"No, unfortunately, it wasn't your killer's blood." Dr. Burke replied with disappointment.

"Then whose blood was it?"

"It was Mrs. Langdon's blood."

"What…how…why." an intensified deeply held sigh emerged and Bridges' breath stopped for a moment to assimilate what she had just heard. "I don't understand. How could that be his wife's blood? She couldn't have moved and put herself in that hideous position."

"The blood was a mixture of Mr. Langdon's and Mrs. Langdon's blood. The only explanation is that the killer must have placed some of Mrs. Langdon's blood in the pool of Mr. Langdon's blood."

"Ok…this is getting stranger by the minute."

"You're telling me. But, I may have some viable information for you," Dr. Burke indicated colorfully again.

"We had an eerily similar case here in Florida about six or seven years ago. It reeked of the same odor and the scene was just as brutal. Unfortunately, the police didn't have enough evidence against their primary suspect," Dr. Burke divulged.

"Really. Who was the primary suspect and did they have any others?" Bridges asked with much anticipation.

"His name was…" Bridges could hear Dr. Burke flipping through pages of what she believed were case files or extensive examination notes and then he continued, "His name was Reginald Hensley."

"Reginald Hensley?"

"Yes. And it looks like he's living in Grosse Pointe, Michigan."

Bridges' jaw dropped and the phone almost slipped through her fingers when she heard the words *Grosse Pointe, Michigan*. *"He is here? In my town or…umm state? Reginald Hensley is here right now?"*

"The last known record of Reginald Hensley shows that he lives at 3125 W. Beaver Rd in Grosse Pointe, Michigan," Dr. Burke replied notably.

"I know exactly where that is, it's on the east side of Detroit just off Lake Saint Clair. I have to call my Captain immediately," Bridges indicated and just before she hung up the phone, Dr. Burke shouted.

"Detective Bridges wait—"

"I'm sorry, Dr. Burke but I've got to call my Captain," she said hurriedly.

"I know, but there's more."

Her heart dropped in the pit of her stomach. She felt as if she would regurgitate her lunch. Her eyes twitched and her speech crumbled to fragments of words, "Wha...uhh...this is. What more is there?"

"That nail you asked about, well, I knew it seemed familiar. The couple that was murdered here in Gainesville, crime scene was fairly similar to the Smits murder. The male victim was found with a big old rusty nail hammered through the palm of his hands. His legs were severed but his arms remained in place. However, his hands were nailed to the floor. The nails measured about six inches long and one inch wide."

Her breathing slowed to a calmer pace, the nail, she thought. It's just about the nail.

"That was about the size of the nail that was hammered into Ronald Smits left hand. The nail has got to symbolize some sort of religious cult or something.

The couple that was killed there, were they religious people?" Bridges inquisitively asked.

"I'm not sure. I would have to pull the police file but the nails would indicate some kind of religious crucifixion or sacrifice. It's almost like—"

Bridges hastily interrupted Dr. Burke's opinion, "It's almost like a painting…"

"A painting? I was thinking more along the lines of—"

Bridges interrupted again, "Thank you Dr. Burke. Thank you. You've been more help than you could ever realize. *I gotta go now. I will call you later.*"

Bridges quickly ended her call with Dr. Burke and tried to call Captain Crawford but there was no answer. Her mind wandered off for a concentrated moment. She thought of the odd paintings at the Smits and Langdon crime scenes. "I need to get my hands on those painting," she whispered. The paintings were bagged into evidence but they were still in the forensic lab awaiting examination, when she last inquired.

Just then, she realized she had made it to her police cruiser but didn't manage to drive off. She glanced across the parking lot and noticed she was still at the station. She hurried from her car, ran across the parking lot and burst through the station doors with mad force and nervousness. The morbid scene inside the station had come alive when Bridges raced to Captain Crawford's office out of breath.

Captain Crawford stood up in a panic and shouted, "Are you alright girl? What the hell is going on?"

Bridges tried unsuccessfully to control her breathing and excitement but the overwhelming nature of this visit had grabbed her by storm. "Captain..." she takes a deep breath, bent over and rested her hands above her knees as if she had run a marathon. "We have a strong lead on the killer."

"Ok...ok, calm down. Walk me through this Bridges. What's the lead?"

Captain Crawford walked around his desk and stood next to Bridges and rested his hand on her back to comfort her and help calm her breathing so she can continue.

"Reginald Hensley is his name. Reginald Hensley," she repeated in a shaky but more controlled voice.

"Ok, Reginald Hensley. What about Reginald?"

"He may be the killer."

Captain Crawford's eyes widened and he looked at Bridges with a fevering expression. "Are you sure?"

"I just spoke to Dr. Burke—"

Captain Crawford unknowingly interrupts, "Who is Dr. Burke?"

"He's the forensic pathologist that I told you about. I sent the Langdon's blood to him and he found a case in Gainesville that was similar to the Smits murder, down to the nailed husband." Bridges finally gets a hold of her breathing and takes another deep breath and continued,

"He said they had a suspect named Reginald Hensley but they were not able to conjure enough evidence to put him away…and guess where he is now."

Captain Crawford smiled and took a good guess, "He's in Michigan."

"You got it baby, 3125 W. Beaver Rd in Grosse Pointe, Michigan. The Doc is faxing over Reginald's driver's license photo as we speak. It's an old photo, but it will give us an idea of who we are after."

"Let's go." Captain Crawford whistled as he grabbed his phone and radioed for SWAT.

It took a matter of minutes, twenty-four minutes to be exact, to get to Reginald Hensley's home in Grosse Pointe. It seemed every cop in the district had the Hensley place surrounded.

As the darkness moved in heavy, SWAT secured their position outside the front door of the Hensley residence. There was no sign of life inside the home but they were dealing with a sophisticated methodical killer so they didn't have the luxury of taking any chances.

A sudden brisk of wind had traveled from the east, forcing those without facial protection to blink rapidly. The wind also blew in an annoying sense of exhilaration and fear. Their eagerness had submerged into an unexpected twist of terror, banishing any confidence they had exhibit before approaching the Hensley residence.

Without warning, an officer proclaimed emphatically, "I see movement."

A delicate wind slipped passed their faces in a dawdling motion as they tried to mentally prepare for the worse. It appeared to be a shadow or figure protruding through the front window, hovering around as if he was waiting for the guest outside his door to vanish. The ghostly chanting heard throughout the crowd was tenacious and cold. It echoed in the breeze and arrived crisp and fresh. The eerie feeling softly maneuvered over the shoulders of the officers.

The magnitude of the energy that wavered through the air had strengthened with every passing second. Some officers were steadfast on meeting the killer and putting a bullet directly in his brain, while others tried to hide their fear and exude strength for their call of duty. The commotion was too loud to bear because most of the officers were concentrating on their irregular heartbeats.

The adrenaline is now racing through their bloodstream, fluid excreted down the side of their faces, while their hands slightly trembled near the trigger of their loaded weapons. They tried to foresee what was lurking inside for them but relinquishing these thoughts sent them in a state of frenzy and panic.

"Reginald Hensley, this is the police, we have you surrounded. Come out with your hands up," the Captain announced from his bullhorn. The stealth approach flew out the window when the police cars arrived with sirens blazing.

Another sharp wind penetrated the air and caused an interruption when Captain Crawford tried to forewarn Mr. Hensley again. As the crowd grew eager and the night fell, the Captain gave the ok for the team to rush in.

The crashing noise of the door being charged had stunned several officers who had missed the go ahead gesture from the Captain because they had been consumed within their own fear. Some officers lagged behind, reluctant to enter the residence of a known maniac.

The officers storm inside, search the premises and found nothing.

"There's no one here Captain."

"Ok...search the place. We are checking for any evidence that may link Reginald to our Vics. Be thorough people. We need hard evidence. We can't let this bastard get away!" Captain Crawford demanded.

Chapter 13

Flushing out Mr. Tom

"HOW IS IT GOING MR. MULLENS?"

"I discovered some very interesting things but I haven't determined who Tom is yet. I may have determined what he wants though," Mr. Mullens replied.

"Please, do tell."

"Oh, before I continue...I also researched the phone number you gave me when Tom first called you and it came up empty. It was a disposal cell and it hasn't been used since."

"I had a feeling you wouldn't turn up anything. Please, go on…"

"It seems that all the murdered Vics have or had an interest in the property that you are trying to procure. I'm still trying to determine how the Palowski's play into this intricate story, but for the most part, your building and land seems to be the main focus."

"Right. I don't know why he would be in the middle of this. I had no dealings with Mr. Palowski or his family," Mrs. Deveraux confirmed. "Mr. Palowski was a very powerful man with influences in the Senate and perhaps even in Congress," she said deprecatingly.

"The FBI is crawling all over the police about the Palowski murders because Mr. Palowski's brother is an FBI agent."

"Really. That is very interesting Mr. Mullens. Why would an FBI agent's brother be mixed up in unscrupulous affairs? There has got to be another angle here. Dig deeper into Mr. Palowski's background and his brother's background too. I want to know all the angles before the next person sneezes, you got that Mr. Mullens," Mrs. Deveraux demanded and ended the call.

MRS. DEVERAUX'S MIND started to wander into disconcerting areas. She had her own list of questions that desperately needed to be answered. She felt she could not see the light through the vast of darkness. It was a feeling she had only felt when she walked into that cold empty house to find her mother brutally murdered. Her images of that day had certainly been altered but she could vividly see the blood. It was so much blood. Over the years she had moved passed the relived nightmares and brash cries that had awakened her. She had moved passed the middle-of-the-night frantic screams for her mother and the perfuse sweating that soaked her bed. She had eventually moved passed the tormenting terror that saturated her mind with countless fears. But nothing could remove the images of the blood. She had become fixated on the blood. Mrs. Deveraux's mother had been dead for hours but in Mrs. Deveraux's mind the blood still poured from her mother's wounds like a leaking faucet.

The repulsive thoughts had concealed her in the dark shadows of that horrific day and she found herself pointlessly sauntering through the day. Mrs. Deveraux could not stop the deep burning thoughts that compelled her to pause with sudden fright. The anguish had settled in the cavity of her stomach and the ghosts moved in.

Up until now, Mrs. Deveraux had found many ways to suppress the volatile nature that smoldered inside her. By systematically taking over another's possessions and evoking power over their being was her therapy. Peerless creatures, is what she would call the trivial people she destroyed during the reign of her storm. Yet, somehow, in the beginning, she had underestimated Tom. Tom was not one of those worthless or bottomless people she had trampled over in the past; he had grabbed her attention and forced her to retrace her steps. She couldn't reject Tom's presence.

With the afternoon sun gleaming across her face, Mrs. Deveraux had truly forgotten where she was headed before receiving Mr. Mullens's call. Her mind had become wrapped around the secret intimate world of *Tom*, that she had displaced her agenda. "Who are you Tom? And what do you want from me?" she asked secretly.

"Why is everyone so interested in *my* land?" She sat behind the wheel of her BMW and deeply pondered over the facts, trying to piece the puzzle together. She knew high powered officials meant FBI and the FBI meant politics. "Perhaps I should give Senator Joy a call to see if he can shed some light on this situation."

"SENATOR JOY, HOW are you on this fine afternoon." The cynicism pierced through the phone with fine toning. Senator Joy was not fond of Mrs. Deveraux but he tolerated her for her money and her connections. Not to mention, she held a deep secret of his.

"Mrs. Deveraux, what do I owe the pleasure of this call," he said with false excitement. Both Mrs. Deveraux and Senator Joy were good at counterfeiting how they felt about one another but their true feelings didn't have to be sniffed out by a bloodhound. Senator Joy rested the top part of the phone receiver on the tip of his forehead and sighed quietly with irritation as he waited for Mrs. Deveraux to respond.

"I'm sure you are a very busy man so I will get right to the point of this call. Do you know Jack Palowski?"

The Senator wanted to lie but he knew Mrs. Deveraux would smell a lie a mile away. His heart thumped for several seconds and after several moments of emptiness on the phone, he responded, "Yes, I believe I do. Jack and Rachel Palowski right? His wife is Rachel?"

"I believe his wife name is Rachel. Anyway, what are you two up to?" she blurted unexpected.

"Umm...I'm sorry, what are you talking about Mrs. Deveraux?" he responded nervously.

"You two must be up to something because you have involved yourself in my affairs," she barked.

"I don't understand." he answered again but with a sincerer tone.

"Don't play politics with me Mr. Joy. You may be the Senator, but I have been at this a lot longer," she said grimly. Her frightening and unnerving stern look could be felt through the phone. The Senator knew she meant business and he had to allay her suspicions.

"Mrs. Deveraux, I have no dealings with Mr. Palowski. My wife and his wife are friends and from time to time we get together at the country club or Jack and I play a short game of golf. I don't know what brought you to this conclusion but perhaps you may need to seek other resources."

"You politicians can talk your way out of anything." Feeling nauseated from the political rubbish he just spouted out his mouth, Mrs. Deveraux placed her hand to her stomach and secretly gagged as if she would vomit. "Remember…I know all your little secrets so don't play with me Mr. Joy."

"Come on Mrs. Deveraux. Why would I be interested in your affairs? What affairs are you referring to anyway?"

"It appears that everyone wants my building and land on the west end of Detroit. I couldn't fathom for the life of me how and why you were involved. It took me a while to put the pieces together."

"And you still have a few pieces to go because I'm not one of the pieces that you're looking for Mrs. Deveraux."

"For your sake, let's hope that you're right Mr. Joy," she warned.

"Trust me Mrs. Deveraux, I have nothing to do with your affairs or your building."

"Of course I don't trust you. Trust is earned not borrowed and you politicians have a way of borrowing the righteous attributes you need to get elected. Have a good day Mr. Joy."

Click.

"Bitch." he said aloud once he heard the dial tone.

AFTER MRS. DEVERAUX hung up the phone, it rang. The ring had startled her and her heart pulsated rapidly when *Restricted* appeared across the screen of her cell phone. She knew it was Tom.

"And what can I do for you today Tom."

"I am impressed. You can feel me now, is that it?" Tom faintly laughed and stated his demands. He didn't want to risk losing another round with Mrs. Deveraux. "I see you are still up to your greedy ways."

"And what—"

Tom cut her words short and continued, "I am warning you Mrs. Deveraux. Stop your dealings now or you will be sorry. I know you think you're the most powerful person in this state but you don't know me. You have no idea what I am capable of," he assertively stated.

"If you even think about burying me Tom, I will pin your balls to the wall," she calmly, yet compellingly injected.

"You've underestimated me Mrs. Deveraux and you will pay for that."

Click.

A blanket of anger covered Mrs. Deveraux's face and for the first time, in a long time, she felt as if she would vomit. She had become sick with not knowing who Tom was and what he was after. She could only assume that he had to be a dark figure from her past that has come to collect her soul. Her nerves were shot and her smugness started to lose its momentum. She had become wrapped around the thought of finding Tom and putting an end to the darkness that she had buried so many years ago.

AN UNMARKED BLACK truck with deep tinted windows pulled up next to Tom's Mercedes Benz. Tom maneuvered out of his vehicle and jumped into the spooky dark SUV.

"A little dramatic don't you think," Tom stated.

"What's the problem," Senator Joy responded.

"Not a problem for me." Tom laughed and so their business commenced.

Senator Joy handed Tom a folded yellow envelope. "Here is the hundred thousand you've requested for your research and here is another three hundred for your trouble."

"And the information on Mrs. Deveraux?"

Senator Joy furnished another yellow envelope filled with documents and photos. "This information just fell into your lap, you got that."

"I know the rules, do you? Cause I don't want you trying to destroy me once this job is finished," Tom said.

"Now why would I want to do that?"

"Because you're a Senator and you don't want to be pulling your ankles if this plan hits the fan. You'll definitely need a scapegoat and that person, I'm sure, would be me."

"But this plan will not blow up in my face because I'm not a part of any plan and I don't know what dealings you're talking about. This is a business transaction, plain and simple. I thought we were here to lobby for a particular policy that you need my influence on," Senator Joy stated defensively.

"Whoa, whoa, calm down Senator. You don't need to answer to me. Both of us have an interest in this deal and I will do what I need to do to make sure Mrs. Deveraux's project is questioned and postponed."

"*No.* I need her *destroyed.*"

"I feel the same but I must do this my way Senator. I know her progress is threatening your funding but she has already taken *everything* from me," Tom stated.

"Yes, she has a way of doing that doesn't she." The Senator looked ahead and for a fleeting moment he was lost in his own thoughts.

Tom gently patted him on the back and said, "Don't worry, I will destroy her and her projects. I might even scare *SoftLine* away." Tom laughed and exited the vehicle.

Tom was just about to walk away and then he stopped all of a sudden. He tapped on the dark tinted window and Senator Joy lowered his window. The window stopped almost half way, partially revealing the

Senator's face. "What's the deal between you and Mrs. Deveraux?" Tom asked.

"Let's just say I have a personal need for her disposal."

Chapter 14

On the Trail of a Killer

WHEN A ROOKIE OFFICER LOCATED THE PICTURES of Ronald Smits and his wife in Reginald's home; Captain Crawford and the team patted the rookie on the back and with a candid smile, the rookie walked off with much delight. It wasn't until the Captain took a second glance at the photo and the face that stared back at him was one of familiarity.

"*Dammit!*" Captain Crawford shouted aloud in disappointment.

"What? What's the problem Captain?" An officer asked with bulging eyes.

"Dammit. I can't believe this shit. This cannot be happening."

"What's the deal Captain?" Det. Jarrod asked hesitantly, fearing the Captain's response.

"*Please tell me this is not Reginald Hensley.*" The Captain finally responded angrily.

"Let me see that." Sgt. Willowbee snatched the 5x7 picture frame from the Captain's hand. Captain Crawford hadn't noticed the abrupt disrespect because he truly wanted an answer to his question. Somehow, he knew it wouldn't be the response he wanted to hear. Sgt. Willowbee studied the photo and came to the same conclusion.

"I'll be damn. This *is* a photo of Ronald Smits *and* his wife. You're right Captain, I recognized them from the crime scene photos," Sgt. Willowbee confirmed.

"I don't believe this. I thought that damn driver's license photo of Reginald looked familiar but it didn't hit me until I laid eyes on this recent photo of Mr. Smits," Captain Crawford stated infuriatingly.

"So, are you saying that Reginald *is* Ronald Smits?" Bridges rhetorically asked.

"This is not good people. With all the man hours that we have spent on this investigation, we should've made more progress than this. We are months into the investigation and still…*nothing*," the Captain indicated in a rasp low steady voice that captured the attention of the officers and detectives in the room.

"We couldn't have known Captain. We followed a lead, and a damn good lead I might add," Bridges said. "It was the best lead that we've had since the investigation and Reginald, *well Ronald Smits*, fit the profile." Speaking matter-of-factly, while trying to console the Captain, Bridges recanted how they fell into this promising lead.

"Yeah, you're right. It's simply disappointing when a horrific case, such as this one, runs cold even before the investigation starts," Captain Crawford blurted and walked out of the house.

It was distasteful to Captain Crawford when he learned that Reginald had changed his identity. He knew that the house had the stench of an unoccupied odor. An all too familiar deserted aroma that massaged the tip of a detective's nose hairs. Cops knew this aroma.

Everyone knew they had their man. Reginald fit the profile and his suspicious behavior in Florida made him the perfect targeted suspect of the investigation.

THERE WAS SOMETHING about the blood results that bugged Bridges. She couldn't understand why Mrs. Langdon's blood was mixed with her husband's. Bridges couldn't determine why the blood seemed different. It seemed as if some of the blood was missing from the crime scene.

Back at the station, Bridges brain started running again, "Ok, Dr. Burke indicated that the victim's blood appeared unusual," Bridges recalled.

"What do you mean unusual? You know what Bridges…I'm still trying to pull myself together, can you give me a minute," Det. Jarrod said with mild irritation, as he briskly walked toward his desk which was in the back of the station near Bridges' desk.

Bridges stayed on his heels, trying to get her point across, "I'm sorry Jarrod. I'm sick of this *maniac* getting the best of us and I'm simply trying to get on the same page as the killer. If we understand his motives behind why he does what he does, then we should be able to catch him; or, at least get ahead of him to try and determine his next move," Bridges replied arguably.

"I know," Det. Jarrod answered and inhaled and exhaled an exhausting sigh. "You're right, but these cases are beginning to get to all of us."

"I understand. Trust me, I understand, but I can't sit and soak in my frustrations and disappointments, I have to keep moving."

Det. Jarrod managed to manipulate a subtle smile and for the first time Bridges noticed his inescapable stare. Had he always looked at her this way, she thought. She holstered the stare for the time being and continued her ranting, "I'm just trying to get some footing here, Jarrod."

"Ok. I'm listening."

"Dr. Burke indicated that the blood stains seemed unusual. It appeared that the killer may have taken Mrs. Langdon's blood and mixed it in with her husband's blood. I believe the killer is taking the victim's blood as a keepsake," Bridges suggested.

"A keepsake, huh," Det. Jarrod replied, stopped, turned to face Bridges and continued with a raised brow, "so our psycho is taking souvenirs. Why would he want to take the blood as a keepsake? What do you propose he's doing with this blood?"

"I don't know yet, but I've been thinking about that. I have a few theories but I haven't made sense of them yet."

"Ok, let's hear 'em." Before Det. Jarrod noticed, he had surpassed his desk as they had made their way to Bridges' desk. Det. Jarrod positioned his body inside Bridges' fragile desk chair while she sat on the edge of her old metal desk. Eyes lit with curiosity, Det. Jarrod folded his arms, tucked his left hand deep into the pocket of his right armpit and leaned back in the chair.

"This may seem strange but—"

Det. Jarrod casually interrupted, "Nothing will probably seem strange to me anymore after reviewing the facts of these cases."

Bridges pressed on, "I suppose you're right. But, as I was about to say, I reviewed the crime scene photos over and over again and noticed some interesting things," Bridges continued while her mind wandered for a brief space in time.

"What interesting things?"

"It's just so weird, I'm not sure if it will make sense to you but here goes: I noticed a few strange art pieces at each crime scene."

"Art pieces." Det. Jarrod narrowed his eyes and appeared perturbed by Bridges' statement.

"*Yes*. Hear me out. I studied art at Cambridge in England and there was something strange about these art pieces," she said convincingly. "Well, art wasn't my major but I needed something else to do to occupy my time."

"Really. Cambridge Bridges," Det. Jarrod replied with a hint of sarcasm.

"I'm not trying to be a smart ass, Det. Jarrod, I'm trying to explain something to you," Bridges fervently replied and continued without skipping a beat. She was use to the snarky remarks and the unruly behavior of most of the men at the precinct. She had learned to move pass their egotistical mannerism and focus on the most important things. "As I was saying, I studied art history and I noticed that there were paintings that appeared out of place at the Smits and Langdon crime scenes."

"Ok, following you so far...*I think*."

"These paintings were not by any artist that I could place at the time so I did some digging but haven't found anything yet."

"What does this have to do with the murders?" Det. Jarrod asked tiresomely.

"I believe the killer may have left the paintings at the crime scene."

"Why would he leave a painting? It doesn't make sense. Then again, nothing in these cases make sense."

"I know, I know. That is one of the things I can't figure out but I know those paintings have something to do with these murders. Mr. Smits was a highly religious man but the painting that was found on his wall was not a typical religious painting. It was almost appalling to religion, as if the paintings were mocking his beliefs."

"Ok, I will entertain this for a moment, but I must say, I still don't see the connection Bridges. Who do you think the paintings were by?"

"That's just it, I think the killer may have painted them or someone close to him is painting them for him."

"What makes you so sure of that?" Det. Jarrod asked with further curiosity.

"I'm not sure, that's why it's a *working* theory. However, from the photos, I can tell that they were painted by an unknown artist not a seasoned professional like Rembrandt or Kandinsky. The artist is good enough to pass as a professional artist, and although I didn't study art extensively or in its entirety, I understood enough to spot the real deal."

"Oh, so you're an art expert now," Det. Jarrod sarcastically stated.

"No, I didn't say that. Let's just say that I don't believe these paintings were painted by any well-known artist. I have not conclusively determined who the paintings belong to but I will," Bridges said with much certainty.

"Ok. All this fuss over a few paintings; please tell me how you think they are related to any of these cases?" Det. Jarrod secretly wanted to walk away but he had been holding a secret of his own. He was fond of Bridges. From her fiery red hair to her sizzling personality; he liked everything about her, except her meaningless chatter of course. He couldn't tell you when it first hit him. He simply looked up one day and found his mind gravitating toward her. He couldn't help it. Even though there were times when he felt compelled to share this desire with Bridges, Det. Jarrod decided to keep this fetish to himself. Besides, he wasn't sure if she felt the same way and he didn't want to risk hindering their partnership.

"The paintings were bold, vivid, and fresh; so that is one reason why I determined they were painted by an amateur or an unpopular artist. But here is where it gets weird; the paintings revealed hints of the crime scene—"

Det. Jarrod swiftly interrupted, "What do you mean? *You should have mentioned this first.*"

"Well, I was trying to put it together as I was telling you. I told you it was a working theory dammit. Cut me some slack."

"What about the crime scene hints? Tell me what you've figured out." Det. Jarrod asked impatiently.

Bridges briskly moved to the other side of her desk and pulled out a few of the crime scene photos. She anxiously spread the photos about the desk and pointed to the first painting that was hanging on the wall at the Smits residence. "Take a look at that painting. Doesn't something seem odd about it?"

"It does appear to be a little out of place but I can't get what you see," Det. Jarrod stated as he zoomed in on the photo, trying to examine it from all angles. He had decided to entertain Bridges. He couldn't see what she had envisioned. The paintings did appear distinct from the other neatly hung paintings but rich people never surprised him with their god-awful purchases.

"Look at the colors, the shadow, and the light. I mean, you don't have to be an artist or an art major to see that something is off about that damn photo Jarrod." she explained excitingly and then added, "this painting has hints of our crime scene with the positioning of the bodies."

"It looks pretty red or burgundy. It does seem a little eerie. And now that you have mentioned it, as you look at the other paintings, this eccentric painting is surely out of place." Det. Jarrod leaned back in the chair as his eyes still scanned the photos scattered across the desk and said, "I can't see the crime scene similarities though…not from these photos, I would need to see the real deal," He paused for a moment and asked, "Ok, what does it mean?"

"I don't know. But, I believe that is our answer. If we find out what the paintings mean or who painted them or where they came from, I think we will have our killer," Bridges said with certainty.

"I don't know Bridges. I don't know."

Both Bridges and Det. Jarrod sit in silence as they try to absorb the theory. Det. Jarrod broke the silence and asked, "So, what were the other theories?"

Bridges laughed comically and said, "My other theories. You already know what they are, the infamous Mrs. Deveraux."

"Oooh, yes, Mrs. Deveraux." Det. Jarrod smiled and nodded his head in sheer fascination. "I can't believe you are still on that. Do you strongly believe that *Mrs. Deveraux* could have mutilated eight people?"

"Did you know that she found her mother brutally murdered when she was a young girl? Her mother mutilated too and it was not pretty."

Det. Jarrod glanced up at Bridges in a changed puzzled expression. "No, I didn't know that," he uttered with surprise.

"Yeah, and one of the cops suspected that Mrs. Deveraux had something to do with the brutal murder of her father. He was practically beheaded when his body was discovered and the case is still an unsolved murder today."

"Wow. You have done your homework Ms. Lady." Det. Jarrod said mockingly.

"Don't call me that. I can take anything off you guys but don't belittle me or disrespect me," Bridges said snappily.

"Ok…ok, I apologize. Don't get so personal."

Bridges looked at Det. Jarrod as if she wanted to smack the shit out of him, but she reframed and simply mumbled, "Men."

"You don't have to be so cynical, it was just a comment."

"Why do you guys insist on alienating me as if I was just some blabbermouth off the streets?"

"We don't undermine you Bridges. Don't think like that."

"It pisses me off sometimes. Most of the time I can ignore your cynicism but lately, you guys have really been under my skin and it needs to stop," Bridges said with a hint of annoyance.

"I really didn't mean to piss you off Bridges. Are you pissed at me?" Det. Jarrod asked in a boyish tone. The last thing he wanted to do was run her away. He had gotten use to Bridges coming to him for advice or a listening ear. He had gotten use to her meaningless chatter and bizarre theories, hell, most of her theories were correct in fact. He had also gotten use to her enchanting smell. Her soft scent he pulled from her freshly shampooed hair, the tantalizing scent from her soft perfume that challenged his composure, and her, *I don't give a shit*, swag that made her real. Det. Jarrod didn't want or need Bridges to be upset with him, especially before he could make his move, if he ever worked up the nerve to ask her out.

Bridges glanced over at Det. Jarrod and there was that look that she had holstered. She thought perhaps she should address it, but then she decided against it. "Whatever, anyway, I still believe Mrs. Deveraux is involved in these murders. She may not be the murderer, but she is involved in some way. There is evidence to suggest that she was the last one to see Ronald Smits and Mr. Holmes before they were murdered. Bank transactions confirm that Mrs. Deveraux, Mr. Smits, and Mr. Holmes had business dealings two days prior to each of their murders," Bridges proclaimed with sureness.

"Ok, let's just say that Mrs. Deveraux is involved in some way, why would she need to kill them?"

"She wants to get her hands on everything. Maybe they wouldn't give in to her demands, I don't know."

"Let's run with that theory. If Mrs. Deveraux is behind the murders, who's the killer? Who do you think could pull off such a crime, elude us, and go undetected?"

"I know you don't want to hear this but Sgt. Willowbee could go undetected — "

Det. Jarrod quickly interrupted, "But he's not a killer Bridges. Come on now. You are going a little too far. I'll need you to come back to earth," he said with great disgust.

"Well, I do believe that he is helping Mrs. Deveraux. She is the piece to this puzzle, I just know it."

"Even if Sgt. Willowbee is assisting Mrs. Deveraux, he is not a killer and I want you to get that through your big brain." Det. Jarrod said forcefully.

"Ok, I will." Now she figured she was pissing Det. Jarrod off.

"Seriously, from all the players involved, from the murdered victims to the people that may have an interest in the building and land that constantly seem to be centered around this unyielding investigation; who do you think would be the killer?"

Bridges and Det. Jarrod silenced for a moment, eyes glued to the emptiness of the air. "Who are the players?" Bridges finally asked.

"Most are dead, but according to the information that I uncovered, Mrs. Deveraux, Mr. Cooper, Mr. Kensington, and a few others may be involved or have an interest in the building and land."

"Mr. Cooper."

"Why him?"

"He ran into a few problems a few years back and I don't believe he recuperated from it," Bridges explained.

"Ok, I can buy that." Det. Jarrod subtly moved his head in agreement. "But why would he need to kill?"

"He's desperate; he needs the money and Mrs. Deveraux makes him a deal that he simply cannot refuse."

"Ok, let's start working these theories. I will look into Mr. Cooper. I will gather as much information on him as I can and you can do your research on those crazy paintings. I would help you with that but my art studies aren't what they use to be."

"Very funny." Bridges and Det. Jarrod laughed while Bridges picked up the photos from the desk, placed them back inside the envelope, tucked them into her top desk drawer and headed out the station.

Chapter 15

A Painting of a Thousand Words

THE IV BAG FILLED WITH SALINE SOLUTION HUNG steadily on one of the four Ram's Horn hooks connected to the IV Stand. The clamps held the Colleague 3 Infusion Pump in place. The infusion pump contained the recombinant plasma treatment needed for his survival. The 3 Infusion Pump was designed for continuous intravenous delivery of medication and he needed just over 2500 U (units) with every injury or episode.

The IV Stand held the infusion pump and a morphine pump that was used to administer morphine therapy treatments for chronic pain. His IV line ran directly into a plump vein over his left wrist. He programmed the machine to administer the medicine as follow: First the saline solution was delivered to his body; next the *Factor VIII Replacement Therapy* factor was administered; and then the pain medication delivered the medication directly to the fluid around the spinal cord for almost instantaneous relief of pressure.

After a few hours had passed and his treatments had subsided, he studied his self-inflicted wounds. As he examined his gash, he could revisit the act. He could visualize the blade deeply penetrating his flesh. An odd puzzling look overwhelmed his face and he turned his head from side to side as if he was trying to see deeper inside the wound.

A sudden jerk snapped him back into reality. He eased up from the comforts of a cozy plush chair, firmly gripped his IV Stand pump handle and slowly made his way to his art studio on the other side of the house.

He entered the doorway of the art studio and took an enormous deep breath. He grinned with much enjoyment and started his ritual. He placed a surgical mask across his nose and mouth; goggles covered his eyes; and thin black latex gloves covered his hands. He was ready.

This was his fifth painting and it was going to be the best one yet, he thought. An unexpected smile drifted in place as he studied the materials he would use. The blood from the previous victims had started to clot inside the tubes so the blood had to be heated to be applied to the painting.

After he applied the gesso sealant to the canvas, he mixed the blood with acrylic paint to enhance the light and dark shadows of his portrait. His paintings had to be realistic, bold, intense, and rich. He had tried to master these skills for some time now and he knew he was almost there.

"My work is going to be undeniable, remarkably fresh, and desired," he uttered. "They can no longer deny me as an artist. My work will be remembered and embraced for decades to come." His horrific laugh infiltrated the air and his monstrous grin revealed evilness.

He opened up a heated vial of blood and dipped his paint brush inside, smeared a test amount of blood onto a piece of loose construction paper and decided that the blood was ready to use. He began his brush strokes but knew he had to move fairly quickly before the air caused the blood to clot again.

BRIDGES EYES WERE glued to the pages of the art books she had checked out of the library. She examined the artists that were similar to the unusual paintings she examined at the crime scenes. After much deliberation, there were three artists that stood out from the rest:

Rembrandt, Bernini, and Caravaggio. She had been familiar with Rembrandt but she didn't know much about the other two, especially Caravaggio. Bridges' gathered all the information she could on the time period of these artists and extensively compared their paintings to the work of her killer. Well, she assumed the killer left the paintings. "Who else could have left them," she mumbled to herself. "I mean, what kind of coincidence that would be for the same unique painting to have been purchased by both of our Vics," she thought.

Bridges closely studied the time period of each artist's work. She stumbled across the Baroque time period that was reflected in Caravaggio's work. As Bridges canvassed the area of paper and books on Caravaggio, it was thought-provoking to her. For an intensified short-lived moment, her attention was deep-seated into the printed pages of Caravaggio's work and life.

Caravaggio was an Italian painter, born Michelangelo Merisi de, who later went by the name of his birthplace, Caravaggio, Italy. The work of Caravaggio and presumably, the killer's resembled, and their paintings seemed to represent the *Baroque Cultural Movement* that took place throughout Western Europe in the 16th Century. The *Baroque* art was rich, deep bold colors, intense light and dark shadows, and filled with over-the-top drama. Bridges noticed this work immediately.

In an instant, Bridges found a painting that mimic one of the paintings found at the crime scene and surprisingly, the painting also reflected subtle hints of the crime scene itself, down to the positioning of the bodies. "What the..." Bridges gasped for a quick second, hand over mouth, as she slowly pulled the photos closer. She grabbed the actual canvas and held it close to her face to try and observe the art work more closely. The crime scene painting had been examined by the forensic team and released to be placed with the other evidence.

She examined Caravaggio's piece titled, *Crucifixion of Saint Peter*, and noticed the strong disturbing resemblance to the painting left at the crime scene. Bridges pulled the book photo of the Caravaggio's painting in closer and scanned her eyes across the nailed left hand that mimicked the nailed hand of Mr. Smits. She scanned the picture further and noticed the left dirty foot of the man kneeling on the Caravaggio painting just as Mrs. Smits's body had been positioned. She was astounded.

Bridges anxiously swept her eyes across the painting that was left at the Smits' crime scene. The peculiar similarities were unnerving. She noticed that the dark areas of the killer's painting were much bolder and the red tones were more vibrant. In the deep indistinct section of the painting, Bridges thought she saw something. She pulled the painting closer for a definitive confirmation. "It appears to be something in this corner…" She drifted her eyes toward the top right corner of the canvas, turned the painting to try and reflect it off the light in the evidence room, and then it hit her. Almost unnoticeable to the naked eye, but certainly visible with intense examination was an exquisite imprint of a woman's face protruding through the bold darkness in the top right corner of the painting. Bridges was blown away. The amateurish ideas she had conjured earlier had vanished after she carefully examined this masterpiece. "He's talented," she whispered and smiled.

She lifted the painting from the Langdon crime scene and found that this painting resembled Caravaggio's *Beheading of Saint John the Baptist*. She also found the same feigned face of a woman protruding through the painting. It was as if her face was reaching out to you and crying for help, Bridges thought. "There has to be some significance with this woman. Who is she?"

Bridges leaned back in the evidence room chair, interlocked her hands and positioned them across the back of her neck. "Where do I go from here?" she secretly asked. She sighed exhaustingly, leaned her head back, hands pressed against the backing of the chair and closed her eyes. She rested her brain for several minutes and then she continued her browse.

As Bridges started to re-examine the crime scene paintings, she noticed it had a weird unique odor. But after several hours of intensive examination, she thought perhaps she was losing it. She held the painting closer and the stench soared through her nose with unresisting force. She blinked twice and snatched the painting away from her face.

"What is that smell? Did they examine this properly?" Bridges looked strongly at the art work and muttered, "What kind of paint is this?" She glanced over the evidence room to see if she could find something to gently scrape the painting with.

Nothing.

She pulled her keys from her pocket and flipped opened a mini size pocket knife, gently scraped away a pen point size of paint from the portrait. She held the knife to her nose and took a whiff. "That is truly an odd smell. There must be something more than paint on this canvas. I have to get this painting back to the forensic lab," she said quickly while gathering up all the evidence. "Did they really miss this obstructive smell? What were they doing with the painting, admiring it?"

Bridges made her way back to the forensic lab and demanded that they do an analysis on the paint. "And figure out what that smell is."

"What are we testing for Det. Bridges?" one scientist asked.

"Everything Boyd," she said hastily. "And I need those results yesterday Boyd." she proclaimed as she rushed out the door.

"Everything," Boyd repeated to himself. "What does she mean by everything? It's a damn painting." Boyd's body demeanor shifted toward irritation and he didn't know where to begin. With one quick glance, he leaned closer to the painting and curiosity set in. "This painting looks weird." He pulled the painting closer and gave it a whiff. "It smells a little strange but that could be from being stored with the other evidence." Boyd stared at the painting for what seemed like an hour, and then he decided to run every test he could think of in relation to the crime scene. "Let's take a sample to see what kind of paint we are dealing with here. Since this was a crime of murder, let's test for blood, paint, sealants, and anything else that comes to mind. I don't want any trouble from Detective Bridges."

BOYD HAD BEEN in shock for the past ten minutes as he tried to wrap his head around his discovery. It had taken more than nine weeks to complete his analysis. He was overwhelmed but excited by his conclusion. He called Bridges immediately.

Bridges couldn't step a foot in the door before Boyd started his explanation. "Ok, I was able to isolate several components to this painting. This is some strange stuff and I didn't believe it at first so I ran a presumptive test and then I ran more conclusive tests that would detect traces of—"

Bridges calmly interrupted and told Boyd to take a deep breath. "Calm down and explain it to me delicately because the technicality of how you arrived at your analysis is not my forte." She smiled and continued, "Now, what did you find out?"

"You will not believe this."

"With this case, I am inclined to believe anything," she said tiresomely.

"Well, the paint on the painting is not paint. Well, it is paint but it's not paint too."

"You've lost me already Boyd."

"Ok, the painting is a mixture of paint in some areas and blood in other areas. In some exclusive areas of the painting, only the blood is present; like in the top right hand corner here." Boyd pointed to the top of the canvas where Bridges had discovered the woman's face. "Now, I was able to pull enough samples from the painting to perform a DNA test. It was challenging and the results are not 100% conclusive because the blood was distorted by the acrylic paint and a sealant. A sealant is primarily used on canvases to preserve the painting from color change or fading."

"I know what a sealant is Boyd. I am actually quite familiar with art, I just need to know about the blood," Bridges indicated. "What in the world is up with the blood and why is there blood on a painting?"

"I was able to isolate DNA from several donors."

"*Donors*. What are you saying? *This painting was painted with blood?*"

"Yes. I can conclusive say that this painting was painted with blood," Boyd confirmed.

"Are any of the donors our Vics?" she asked inquisitively, fearing Boyd would say *no*.

"Unfortunately, no. However, the blood was a mixture of a several profiles but I only got one hit from CODES."

"You gotta be shitting me."

"Not sure if the hits will help but perhaps it will give you an area to examine or a place to start," Boyd replied with reassurance.

Bridges chuckled, shook her head in disbelief, and said, "I don't think we are ever going to figure out this damn case. Everything keeps getting stranger by the minute."

"The blood was from three potential donors. Well, I believe I was able to isolate three different DNA profiles. Two were male and one was female. The other unfortunate aspect is that one of the male profiles shows he's deceased. According to the hit in CODES, he died from complications of the liver from hepatitis."

"*Hepatitis?* What is *really* going on around here Boyd?"

"Also—"

Bridges interrupted again and softly whispered, "I don't know if I can handle anymore Boyd." She located the only seat in the lab and flopped down with useless energy. "What else have you got?"

Before Boyd could respond to her question, she asked another, "Why was he in CODES anyway?"

"Prostitution, drug possession, and a few misdemeanors, nothing elaborate and definitely nothing as peculiar as this," Boyd replied.

"Neither one of those crimes remotely fit into our cases, this is unbelievable," Bridges said and continued, "What else you got?"

"The other male profile was stronger than the other profiles. Actually, it was the strongest of all the profiles, yet it was something faint about his blood. I ran a blood analysis test to determine his blood type and if there were any abnormities in the blood but I couldn't get a definitive answer. But there is something different about his blood that our lab wasn't able to detect."

"What if you examine the other painting?"

"*What other painting?*" Boyd inquisitively asked.

"The painting we retrieved from the Langdon crime scene." Bridges pulled out a small notepad and rattled off the evidence trace number, "Article number PS39-12. I sent it down after I left your lab that day. I realized that I had only brought down the Smits crime scene painting so I sent the Langdon painting down soon after my return to the evidence room. It should be here. Perhaps one of your colleagues has it."

"I should check. I will locate the other painting and run a full analysis as I did with this painting," Boyd promised.

"That's fine. Call me when you get the results."

"It will be my pleasure."

Bridges got the distinct feeling that Boyd, the geek, was starting to enjoy this. "At least someone is getting some excitement out of this because we are digging ourselves a hole so dark and deep that I'm not sure if we can come back from this," she mumbled to herself on her way out the door.

Chapter 16

A Building of Interest

"WHAT IS SO URGENT THAT YOU HAD TO PULL me out of bed?" Bridges groggily asked Boyd, forgetting that she had asked him to call her once he had analyzed the painting from the Langdon crime scene.

"You won't believe this, but maybe you will, I don't know but it's crazy but amazing at the same time, it—"

Bridges slowly awaken and interrupts Boyd's babbling, "Wait, wait, wait Boyd. Calm down and start all over."

Boyd takes a deep breath. "I analyzed the other painting and found blood. No surprise there; however, it was whose blood I found that is the surprising factor."

"Who?" She asked while holding an entangled expression across her face.

"I ran the blood sample through the system and one of the donor's came back to a missing person's case from fifteen years ago—"

The anticipation was killing Bridges, she interrupted again, "Who Boyd? Who is the donor?"

"Wendell Thomas Grimshaw." Feeling a sense of excitement and accomplishment, Boyd took a deep breath, sighed in relief and smiled with delight.

"*You gotta be fuckin' kidding me!* What is going on around here?" By this time, Bridges is sitting up in her bed, head rested along the headboard, as the hand that held her cell phone flopped effortlessly to her lap.

Minutes had passed and Boyd called out for Bridges. *Nothing.*

"Hello, Bridges, are you still there?"

"Yeah…yeah Boyd, I'm here. This case is unbelievable. This is like some kind of nightmare movie that we can't awake from. Are you sure it was Wendell Grismshaw?"

"Yes. I sent samples to a forensic anthropologist to confirm my findings. That's why it took a little longer than before. At the University Center for Biological Testing, Dr. Meek was able to concur with my findings."

"What are we supposed to do with this darn evidence now?" she said with drained energy. She bit down on her lip, trying to contemplate her next move.

"Well, what do you know about his disappearance? Maybe you can start by pulling his case file and determine who wanted him dead. I mean, this is not enough blood to determine that Mr. Grimshaw is deceased but it could get you a warrant for any persons of interest," Boyd added confidently.

Bridges eyes sparkled with intensity and she replied, "Thank you Boyd. You are the best. I know just who we need to question."

"CAPTAIN, PLEASE TELL me you still don't believe that Mrs. Deveraux is innocent." Bridges said in disappointment.

"I never said that Mrs. Deveraux was innocent of anything. We simply need to be cautious. We don't need her kind of trouble right now. You bring me more evidence and I will personally walk to Judge Chambers's office and have him execute a warrant for her arrest. But in the meantime, *no one – I mean no one*, is to speak to Mrs. Deveraux under any circumstances. Do I make myself clear Det. Bridges?"

"Clear as rain Captain."

"Rain is sometimes hard to see through Bridges. I need it to be crystal clear like the specific clear tones you hear during a hearing examination," Captain Crawford reiterated.

"I got it Captain. I got it," she shouted while leaving his office.

"I hope you got it because I would hate to have your badge because of insubordination."

"Ok Captain."

As Bridges started to walk toward her desk, Sgt. Willowbee called out to her.

"Hey, Sgt. Willowbee, we really need to re-visit all the crime scenes again. I have been—"

Sgt. Willowbee interrupts and states, "You should stop trying to question Mrs. Deveraux. The Captain will never allow it and we seriously don't need that kind of trouble."

"What trouble is everyone talking about? And why is everyone protecting her? She's a possible killer Sergeant. We swore to uphold the law, not hide criminals behind it," she barked impatiently.

"We're not sure she's broken any laws and second, we're not hiding her. We need to go easy on this one Bridges. You don't know what this department went through with that woman."

"Enlighten me."

"Come on now. Let's not do this. Just let it go until you have *two legs* to stand on," he calmly begged.

"She is a suspect. We are supposed to question suspects."

"She's a suspect in your book but you have no strong physical evidence to link Mrs. Deveraux to these horrific crimes. And do you seriously think she could have killed a man and cut his legs off. Let's be realistic here." Sgt. Willowbee pointed out with a smirk.

"Don't act as if I'm some sort of rookie cop fresh off the beat. I am so tired of *my fellow officers* not taking me serious. Can you set your ego aside and see that I may be on to something here?"

"It's not my ego that causes my hesitation, its Mrs. Deveraux's wrath that paralyzes you." Sgt. Willowbee zoned out into the clouds again and Bridges recognized that look and déjà-vu sat in. She found herself held deep inside Sgt. Willowbee's concentration and for several short-lived minutes she had zoned out too.

Sgt. Willowbee slightly shook his head and insisted, "Leave it alone Bridges. Just leave it alone."

"She's a suspect Sgt. Willowbee," she firmly replied.

"What evidence do you have that implicates Mrs. Deveraux?"

"First, there was blood evidence found at the Oxford Langdon crime scene that belonged to Wendell Grimshaw. *You know…the billionaire that has been missing for over fifteen years.*" She watched Sgt. Willowbee's obscured reaction and continued, "There were other DNA contributors found at both the Smits crime scene and the Langdon crime scene. Mrs. Deveraux was the last person to see both victims alive before their death and she was in a heated court battle with Mr. Grimshaw before his disappearance." She paused for a moment to take in Sgt. Willowbee's sterile facial expression. Bridges didn't know what to think of such a look but she kept on talking, "Now, in the real world, would you consider the fact that we have more than probable cause to question Mrs. Deveraux?"

"Yes, you are right." He paused. "But we are in our world and Mrs. Deveraux would chew us up and spit us out with that circumstantial evidence. You are on to something here Bridges, I will give you that; but you have to tread lightly or you will find yourself in the midst of a raging river."

Bridges rolled her eyes and sighed in frustration.

"Don't be like that Bridges. I am just warning you to take it easy and be sure to dot all your 'I's' and cross all of your 'T's' because this woman is no ordinary powerhouse. Trust me, you don't want to feel a *subtle hint* of her wrath…it's lethal."

Sgt. Willowbee deeply roots his words into her mind and turned to walk away.

"I'm just trying to find a killer Sergeant. Who are you trying to find?" she shouted as Sgt. Willowbee walked out of the station doors with no response.

BRIDGES FELT SHE was on to something. She had a feeling that someone was covering for Mrs. Deveraux and her assumptions would be challenged with the latest murdered victims.

It was that tingle of fear that ripped through the detectives' bodies as they walked into another blood bath. The Kensington home had been just like the others. William Kensington had been shot at close range, arms and legs removed while the wife had been repositioned just as the other wives.

Bridges was looking for two things: the blood and out of place portraits or paintings. Normally, Bridges would be very particular about the people stepping all over her crime scene but she had been consumed by another mission. She slowly examined the scene, eased around vital evidence, and made her way to Mr. Kensington's study.

"What are you doing in here?" Her first wave of emotion had stunned her and then intrigue set in and she impatiently waited for a response that was not forthcoming.

Sgt. Willowbee glanced up at Det. Bridges with suspicious eyes and continued his browse.

"Are you going to answer me?"

"I don't believe I owe you an explanation *Detective*." Bridges couldn't see the fear and tumult that danced in the pit of his stomach. Bridges had only the first alarming reaction to hold on to as her gut feeling told her something was out of place. She couldn't have known that Sgt. Willowbee had been taken aback as he had been searching for more documents for Mrs. Deveraux.

"But why are you in this room?" she guardedly asked again.

"I could ask the same question of you. Everyone is here working this crime scene so why would my presence be disquieting to you," Sgt. Willowbee said in an eerie tone; a tone that Bridges had never heard before.

"Is there a problem Sergeant?"

"That would be my question to you *Detective*. Yes, *Sergeant*, and you should remember that." He moved away from the Kensington desk, walked over to Bridges, stood close to her and positioned his face near her left cheek and whispered, "You don't get to question me young lady."

The blood had rushed from Bridges face to her toes as she stood in disbelief. She had never heard the Sergeant speak to her or anyone in that manner. It was like something had possessed his body. He was calm, precise, and seemingly diabolical. It engrossed her.

"He's involved," she softly whispered to herself, still standing in the same position. "I can't believe I missed this. No, I didn't miss this, I didn't want to believe it." Bridges stood in the Kensington study in silence until a distant noise had frightened her.

She turned around sharply to face the office door. She waited for the noise to reveal itself but nothing. She gradually took two steps closer to the doorway. A frightening energy had consumed her and a jolted fear had suspended her movements. Bridges wasn't one to scare easily but the weird spin of these events had caused some fretfulness among the officers and detectives. Nothing is what is seemed to be, Bridges thought.

Bridges' mind started to race and the blood that suddenly rushed from her face had disappeared entirely. She took another step closer to the door opening but hesitated before the fourth step. She heard the noise again. She couldn't understand why she was uneasy because the Kensington home was crawling with cops and the noise she heard could just as well be one of them.

Bridges saw an approaching light from the left, outside the office doorway. She imagined the killer appearing in front of her, slicing her neck and vanishing in the wind. Her abrupt trance of an unconceivable daydream was interrupted by Det. Jarrod who had made his way down the hall to the Kensington study.

"I figured I would find you in here," Det. Jarrod said as he subtly laughed.

Bridges, trying to pull herself together replied, "Yeah, and how you figured that?"

"When you told me about those damn paintings and the new evidence you found, I figured you would be here looking for another painting. Did you find one?"

"Not yet. Help me look," she said, trying to divert Det. Jarrod's attention off of her. She was afraid that Det. Jarrod would see right through her. She contemplated if she should tell Det. Jarrod about Sgt. Willowbee but she decided against it. She had to know who all was involved. She couldn't trust anyone.

Meanwhile, back at the station, Det. Popper received a call from Mr. Cooper of *Cooper Construction and Excavation Company* indicating that he wanted to report unauthorized digging at the Mid-Corner Building in Detroit off West Lasher Road, zip 48234.

"Ok Sir, we will send an officer right out," Det. Popper assured. She had wondered why Mr. Cooper would call the Bloomfield Hills Police Department instead of calling the Detroit Police; but then she recalled Bridges indicated that all matters concerning these cases would be directed to their precinct. She hadn't pieced together how or why Mr. Cooper called her line directly but she didn't have time to chew on it too long. Instead of dispatching a patrol car, she decided to check it out herself.

As Popper headed out to the building site, she remembered that Bridges had mentioned something to her about Mrs. Deveraux having an interest in a building and land site. Popper reached for her cell phone and called Bridges.

"Hey, where is that building and land site of Mrs. Deveraux's that you mentioned earlier?"

"It's off Lasher Road, why?"

"Cause we've got a problem out there."

"What sort of problem?" Bridges words released slow but her insides twitched with eagerness.

"Mr. Cooper called me and stated that someone had tried to do some digging."

"Mr. Cooper…digging…why?"

"Hey, your guess is as good as mine. I am going to check it out now."

"Popper…call for backup," Bridges firmly insisted.

"Why? It's just a building site. Some kids may have been playing around the construction site, that's all," Popper replied.

"Please, Popper, call for backup. These cases are getting crazier by the minute and it could be the killer or a set-up. *Don't take any chances with this, call for backup, please*." Bridges beseeched.

"Ok, ok…I will call for backup," Popper agreed with a wide smile. "You have got to relax Bridges. I will check it out, it's probably nothing."

"I will meet you at the building site as soon as I am done here. It shouldn't be too long, I'm just wrapping up. These murders are getting harder to stand. I'll explain when I see you."

"You don't have to meet me at the building, I'm sure it's nothing."

"Whatever…see you in an hour."

Chapter 17

The Suspects

BRIDGES FINALLY MADE IT TO THE BUILDING SITE two hours later. Her vehicle headlights tussled with the obscurity of the night. Bridges drove over the gravel, pass the no trespassing sign, and up a slanted hill where she found Popper's police cruiser. She had to assume it was Popper's because all detectives drove the same standard black sedan.

Bridges pulled over her vehicle, put the car in park and proceeded with caution. She pulled her gun from her holster and unclipped her flashlight from her belt. She securely aimed the gun and the light at Popper's vehicle and quickly searched inside.

No sign of Popper.

Bridges quickly glanced over the immediate area with her gun and flashlight in hand. The chill from the night air buried itself inside Bridges body and a cold crisp fright had settled in her throat. Bridges swallowed hard and took several steps away from Popper's vehicle in a search to find her.

She eased her feet along the gravel, while moving her gun and light to search her surroundings. Bridges could only hear the crunch from her footsteps but even that was uneasy.

Her flashlight moved over a few objects on the ground and suddenly, rooted into the darkness was a disturbed area. Bridges swiftly moved in closer to the disturbed area and found what appeared to be two bodies lying in the partially makeshift grave. She whipped her light frantically to the right and then back to the left.

She paused. She thought she heard a noise in the distance.

She turned to move the light back toward the police vehicles.

Nothing.

She turned back around to face the dug up dirt and what appeared to be two motionless bodies. Then a burst of wind spontaneously flew past her face. She inhaled a gruesome down-reaching breath and her feet slid from underneath her. Bridges recklessly scrambled to find her light that flew from her hands as her body hit the pavement.

She was terror-stricken.

Bridges located the flashlight, bounced back to her feet and anxiously scanned her surroundings again in search of the sudden gust of wind.

It was a bird. "Dammit." she muttered to herself.

Bridges moved in closer to the disturbed dirt and confirmed that it was two bodies in the dirt. It was hard to make out who the victims were but she could only assume one was Popper. "Damn you Popper; why didn't you call for backup." Bridges glanced over the bodies from a distinct distance until she could unequivocally confirm that the area was secure. She made a decision. She had no time to lose in the event that Popper may still be alive.

She ran over to the bodies, quickly scanned the area of the dirt and brushed the debris from the woman's face. It was Popper and she was dead. It appeared that her throat had been slashed.

Bridges glanced back up into the night air to be sure no one was moving toward her. She reached into her pocket for her cell phone. She called it in.

IT HAPPENED WAY before the movie started. It happened before the Coopers had burned the midnight oil. It happened just before the celebration began. It was around five p.m. when the first blow hit. Mitch couldn't have seen it coming but Carol was too stunned to move. You could see the dusty yellowish glow from the rising sun beam through the Cooper's master bedroom window, squinting at Carol's white purplish and pale cheeks as she lay diagonally across the master bed. Her eyes were slightly opened and had stiffened with the passing hours. Decomposition had settled. Her lips were dark blue and purple. She was shot at point-blank range.

Carol was found on the master bed but Mitch's body was missing. Mitch's legs had been severed and placed on the floor at the foot of the bed next to his arms which had been cut off too. The killer had removed Mitch's body from the house for some reason. Perhaps the killer was disturbed by someone or something. Perhaps he was startled by a voice or a muttered sound of some sort, Det. Jarrod decided. It was hard to tell, but it stopped the killer in his tracks. The killer had not neatly lined the body parts up as he had done before.

Mitch was ambushed by the assailant and forced to concede as a 9mm Beretta penetrated his temple. Within seconds, the killer forced Mitch inside the house as he came from his afternoon jog; shoved him onto the living room leather sofa and shot him between the eyes.

The blast pierced through Carol's ears as she frightfully rushed to the top of the spiral staircase. She saw the killer hovering over her husband with inquisitiveness. Carol watched for a moment as the killer seemed mesmerized by the blood that slowly ran from the gaping hole in Mitch's head. He seemed overwhelmingly occupied by the slow puffs of breath that Mitch took as his body slipped into death. At first, he didn't see her, but the noisily gasp that released from her body took the killer out of his spell and focused his eyes on her. She nurtured her mouth with a delicate touch of her hand and immediately dashed for the master bedroom. The killer quickly ran up the stairs in search for Carol. The killer entered two other rooms before finding Carol balled into a corner of the master bedroom. She was too shocked to put up a fight.

She never heard the gun shot blast. She didn't feel the bullet penetrated through her flesh. She only saw flashes of life in full view as if she was watching a movie. She pictured the first time she danced with her husband, in the Greenwich Ballroom of the Valley View Country Club. She could still see the romantic sparkle that shinned in his eyes as he stared into hers.

She couldn't smell the flesh that burned in her chest from the powerful bullet that ripped her skin apart. Her mind had nearly escaped that scent. Instead, what flowed through her nose was the enchanting aroma of the rare Bird of Paradise floral arrangement that Mitch surprised her with the night before this horrific event. Suddenly, her mind had clasped with her body and soon she would fade into a deep dream that would last forever.

"NOW, THIS SHIT is getting personal people. One of our own is dead and we don't have any more time to waste with this bastard. *Find him!*" Captain Crawford hissed. "Bridges...in my office."

Bridges stepped into the Captain's office with shock still distributed across her face. She felt intoxicated from the overwhelming events of the night and her uneasy feeling had turned to ripples of fear. Bridges felt that her steps to this point seemed like objectionable blunders and the only person that had moved ahead was the killer. Seeing the mutilated body of Mr. Cooper partially buried next to Popper was overwhelming. Bridges wondered why the killer removed the body from the house and placed it at a construction site.

"We're stationary Captain. We haven't moved," she murmured.

"Bridges, you've got to get a hold of yourself. We'll catch this bastard. Now...tell me everything that you have uncovered, including your suspicions about Mrs. Deveraux."

Bridges eyes glanced up at Captain Crawford and the word "finally" arose from the smoke of a burning flame. Bridges started with her tedious story of how she came to suspect Mrs. Deveraux: the blood evidence that indirectly links Mrs. Deveraux to the crime thanks to the new found blood evidence of Mr. Grimshaw; the mysterious blood paintings that reeked of eerie similarities to an artist named Caravaggio, including the posing of the wives bodies; Mrs. Deveraux was the last to see each victim alive before their untimely death; and the most unambiguous factor is her mother's brutal death.

"I see. You have been very busy. How does Mrs. Deveraux's mother's death play into this suspicion?" Captain Crawford asked.

"When her mother was found murdered, Mrs. Deveraux's father was the primary suspect and later they found him murdered. He was beaten beyond recognition and almost decapitated. The M.O. rings a bell."

"I see…"

"Captain, even if she didn't pull the trigger, I still feel that she is connected to these murders in some way. I am asking that we bring her in for questioning. She has gotta know that we know something and that we realize these murders are not simply a coincidence," Bridges pleaded.

"I understand. Let's put a round-the-clock tail on her. I wanna know her every movement but don't let her see you. I am going to dig into the budget and get you an inconspicuous rental so you guys won't stick out like a sore thumb."

"You guys…"

"Yes...you and Det. Jarrod. You two seem to be closer to the case than anyone else and I trust that you can bring the suspect in."

"Thank you Captain."

"For what?"

"For believing in me," Bridges said with much appreciation.

"I always believed you and I knew you would find what we needed to move forward on this. This is a very sticky situation with Mrs. Deveraux and we have to do this strictly by the book."

"I always do things by the book Captain," Bridges assured.

"This is different Bridges. Mrs. Deveraux is very powerful and like it or not she has powerful influence over this town and state. We can't afford to make any mistakes or she walks. I've seen it happen before," Captain Crawford said while mumbling that last statement under his breath.

Bridges wanted to press the issue further but she decided to leave it alone. She stood up from the guest chair in Captain Crawford's office and turned to head toward the door. She stood bewildered when her eyes were fixated on the untouchable Mrs. Deveraux standing in the center of the station next to two men that looked like the president's men. Bridges turned to glance at Captain Crawford and his stunned reaction did not go unnoticed.

"What is she doing here?"

"I don't know but we definitely need to find out," Captain Crawford stated with certainty. He maneuvered from behind his desk and headed toward his office door. In the same motion, Mrs. Deveraux moved just as swiftly to greet the Captain.

"Captain Crawford, we have a problem," Mrs. Deveraux proclaimed.

"We've had a problem for quite some time Mrs. Deveraux," he sarcastically replied.

"I may be in grave danger Captain Crawford."

"Is that so…"

"You sound as if you don't believe me."

"Everyone seems to be dying around you, why wouldn't I believe you?"

"This is not a joke, Captain Crawford and I expect the same consideration that you have given to the deceased," she hissed.

"Unfortunately Mrs. Deveraux, I can't give you the same consideration because they're dead. And let's face it, you have never been given the same consideration as anyone in this town," Captain Crawford reminded her and then continued, "now, how can we help you Mrs. Deveraux?"

"I want to know what you are doing about this monster who has invaded our town," she answered.

"We are doing everything that we can to find the perpetrator," Captain Crawford assured.

"Well, what can I do to help? We have got to find him because this travesty has got to end."

"You can start by helping us out with some information," Captain Crawford said matter-of-factly.

"What information?"

"It appears that the killer may be targeting everyone that may have an interest in that building and land you have on the west end of Detroit. We need a list of all your accomplices...I mean your acquaintances," Captain Crawford replied with a smile. Bubbling inside from the smart insinuation he proposed.

"I am going to ignore your brief brain malfunction as you may have forgotten who you are speaking to; but I will be more than happy to give you a list of names. After you read my list, you will see why I fear for my life. Five of the eight people are dead." She handed him a folded white piece of paper.

Captain Crawford scanned the list and pointed out to Mrs. Deveraux that Mr. Copper's butchered body was found partially buried at her building site just a few hours ago. He wasn't convinced that her dramatic response wasn't rehearsed. Manipulation was one of her strongest attributes. He scanned the list again and noticed that Mr. Palowski wasn't on the list.

"Is this the complete list of names?"

"Yes, why?"

"You said that there were eight names, I only see seven."

"The eighth person is *me* Captain," she said, softly speaking in that desirable sophisticated tone that melted men's hearts. She was rather irresistible and her unforgettable eyes pierced through your soul.

"So…are you asking for around-the-clock security for you and this other person on your list?"

She dimly laughed and delicately positioned her hand across her bosom and replied, "It is the killer you should be worried about."

"But you said that you feared for your life," Bridges added.

"Oh dear, but I do fear for my life. It's because I fear for my life that I'm on high alert. I came to you as a courtesy. I will not be taken down dear. So, anyone that poses a threat to me will have a problem. I just thought you should know that…*in the event something happens.*" Mrs. Deveraux winked her right eye at Bridges, embraced her with a warm smile and turned to head toward the doors of the station.

"You can't take matters into your own hands Mrs. Deveraux," Captain Crawford shouted as she walked out the station doors without responding.

"She is up to something Captain," Bridges proclaimed.

"I know. Hell…she's always up to something."

"WHAT IS IT Mr. Mullens?" Mrs. Deveraux asked with grave concern. She heard the terror in his voice when he released his first sentence.

"It's about your husband," Mr. Mullens feverously said.

"*Clayton…what about my husband? Is he alright?*" she asked seeking quicker responses.

"I found some hidden things in his past that you are not going to like."

"Oh, is that all. Dammit, you scared me half to death. Everyone has hidden things in their past Mr. Mullens, why should my husband be any different."

"Mrs. Deveraux…well…your husband is not who he say he is. His last name was Gericault."

"And…"

"Gericault was the other suspect named in your mother's murder. Your husband is originally from London, just as you and he had a violent past. He was also implicated or thought to be the *Florence Butcher*."

Mrs. Deveraux was indeed surprised but she was not threatened. She had already determined who had killed her mother and nothing or no one else would convince her otherwise. Nevertheless, she couldn't hide the overwhelming nerves that jumped through her skin. "Could he be the killer behind these horrific cases?" she asked herself.

"Mrs. Deveraux, are you still there?"

"Yes. What else did you find out Mr. Mullens?" she calmly replied.

Surprised by her cool nature, Mr. Mullens couldn't help but ask, "Were you aware of this information before now?"

"No, I must say I was not. But please go on and explain your other findings," she replied in a calmer manner than before. It was unnerving and Mr. Mullens feared he had gotten himself caught inside a tangled web of lies and deception and the truth was just as incongruous as the inflated fantasies that each character possessed.

"Well, your husband changed his name and moved to the States. There is evidence that he visited a psychiatric hospital but I wasn't able to determine if he was a patient or an employee. It looks like he made most of his money working for organized crime bosses in New York and Boston. Most of his business dealings now are legitimate but I believe he still utilizes his old connections in Boston. I am waiting on a few phone calls and following up on a few leads, so I should know something within the next few days regarding your husband's hospital stay.

"Oh, and I may have a lead on Tom. Everything that I'm finding out leads me back to your building site. What is so special about this darn building site anyway?"

"It's mine, that's what it is and I will not be outdone."

"Do you really think this is about you being outdone?"

"Just know that I will do whatever it takes to hold on to what is mine. No one will stand in my way Mr. Mullens, *no one!*"

A creepy chill ran down Mr. Mullens' spine as her words penetrated his being. He knew behind all that seductive beauty, there laid a woman in shattered pieces. He could feel the wretchedness of her discomfort but her ghastly power poured through you like rain and you soon forgot about any empathy that you may have had for Mrs. Deveraux.

"I will let you know when I find out more," he finally replied.

"Please do…"

Without notice, she hung up.

Chapter 18

What Lies in the Dark

THE GUNSHOT BLAST DRUMMED THROUGH THE AIR like lightning. Before Clayton realized what had happened, he felt a burning sensation in his chest. Seconds later, he doubled over in excruciating pain. The wound was first masked with numbness and then another explosion of pain hit him like a freight train. Disorientation engulfed his mind while the pain plowed through his body. Clayton was breathless.

As he tried gasping for words, his mouth filled with a warm liquid. Once his balancing had been compromised, he tumbled over onto the nearest chair.

His body hit the floor with a hard thump and the blood that was building inside his mouth was released onto the marble floor.

Through his struggled breath and blood filled mouth, Clayton managed to speak, "Why would...you do this...to me?" He started to choke. The internal bleeding from the piercing bullet suffocated his lungs, and his heart ached with anguish. He could not believe what had just happened.

As Clayton lied on the floor, gasping for his last breath, he looked up at his wife and asked again, "Why?"

Mrs. Deveraux glanced down at her husband with little compassion and answered, "You know why."

"Please...tell me," he struggled to say.

"I hear you've been keeping secrets from me," she whispered, as she kneeled next to his convulsing body. A weak smile drifted in place as she watched her husband slip into an agonizing death.

"I...don't...know what...you— "

"Please, stop dear. You should've known that I would find out. I always do. I will *not* let you stop me. Did you follow me here from London?"

His eyes bulged and he started to choke uncontrollably. His casual slip into death abruptly disrupted by his wife's startling question. "No, I didn't...and...and..."

"So, you like going around mutilating bodies," she whispered in Clayton's ear.

"Dear...I...don't...understand," he managed to say.

"Don't play games with me darling. You're that serial killer and it was in your plans to kill me, isn't that correct my darling," she whispered again.

He coughed up more blood and in an effort to spit, the blood that filled his mouth only made it to the tip of his chin. His lungs were collapsing and his body no longer had the strength to carry out his tasks. "You were never...in...my plans. I had to leave...London. I was in...trouble...my...life...was..." And with those last words, Clayton's life slipped away.

Mrs. Deveraux glanced down at her husband's body. She felt duty-bound to hold his body close until it cooled but she decided against it. Her love she felt for her husband could not get in the way of her mission. She wasn't sure if he was *Tom*, but she had her suspicions. It was ironic that her husband had been conveniently out of town when she received her phone calls from the infamous Tom. She didn't find it coincidental that he followed her here from London. She didn't feel it was a coincidence that Clayton was a suspect in her mother's brutal murder.

She had no choice, she kept telling herself.

"We always have a choice. Some of the choices we make, life won't let you forget," she whispered to herself. For a fleeting moment, a somber look absorbed her face. She suddenly felt a solitude that could not be explained. A hint from the moonlight that shined through their dining room window had captured a glare in her water filled eyes. She allowed a tear to escape as she gently rubbed her fingers across the top of his head. She wouldn't allow anything more.

Mrs. Deveraux pulled her body from the floor and reached across the dining room table for her cell phone.

"SHE IS CLAIMING self-defense," Captain Crawford indicated.

"Come on Captain, you know and I know that it was not self-defense. *She is tightening up all her loose ends,*" Bridges exclaimed.

"You may be right Bridges but the evidence points to self-defense. She hired a private investigator; he dug up old dirt on Mr. Deveraux; she questioned him about it and it got ugly...*case closed.*"

"*Captain.*"

"Case closed Bridges. Did you see the photos, Bridges?" Captain Crawford asked in aggravation.

"Yes, I did."

"There was a lot of incriminating evidence just on the photos alone; do you really want to go there with her? *I don't.* She would beat this – hell, I would beat this case. *Let it go Bridges. Self-defense.*" Captain Crawford shouted across the station, stepped into his office and slammed the door.

Bridges' phone rung and without delay, she answered it sharply, "Hello."

"Hi, is this Detective Margret Bridges?"

"Yes, this is she."

"My name is Madeline; I am calling from the European Art Institute in St. Carol. You needed information on a former student, Thomas Grimshaw or one of similar name, yes?" the lady with the French-English accent stated.

"Yes, I did. I do. Do you have a student by that name or did you have a student?"

"Yes, we did. I am sending you over the information now."

"Do you have a student photo of Thomas? Or was his name Thomas?"

"Actually, we only have one student with name Thomas Grimshaw. He was a student for two years and then he just disappeared. We still have some of his personal items in storage at our campus."

"Is there any way that we can see what you have? I mean, would it be possible for you to forward his belongings to us?"

"I thought you may want them so I started the paperwork. Please check email and you will have necessary documentation for release. Please, you must pay for shipment to you."

"Of course, we can do that."

alina

* * *

THE JUDGE ORDERED another excavation of the entire building site. With all the new-found interest and the discovery of Mr. Cooper and Det. Popper's bodies found on the land, the authorities figured there had to be something buried underneath this web of deception.

After a thorough examination of the area, human remains were found. Three to be exact. The authorities were overwhelmed, the media was in frenzy, and the mayor had lost his patience. They felt trapped in the theater of a bad movie that no one could escape from.

The site of the dirty bones lying across the evidence table in the forensic lab was something no detective in this town had ever seen before. But nothing in these cases were normal. It became harder and harder for the detectives to connect the dots.

It took some time but the bones discovered at the building site belonged to Wendell Thomas Grimshaw III, his wife, and his daughter. It appeared that all victims had been beaten to death. The medical examiner concurred that Mr. Grimshaw was overkill. Most of the bones in his face were broken and his skull had been smashed in. A forensic facial artist had to put the pieces of the skull together to even determine if it were a skull before they could conclusively identify the remains.

"We have to comb the Grimshaw Estate, Captain, and guess who owns it now." Bridges gloriously indicated.

"Of course, *Mrs. Deveraux*. I will get the court order."
Captain Crawford said.

"BODIES FOUND AT *a well-known building site have been
determined to be Wendell Thomas Grimshaw III and his loving
wife and daughter. Grimshaw had been missing for over fifteen
years. You may know the Grimshaw name through several
public court hearings involving Mrs. Julie Ann Deveraux, one
of the most elite and powerful women of our town. Mrs.
Deveraux was granted full control of the Grimshaw Estate and
awarded all rights.*

"*Mrs. Deveraux's latest court hearings were over this
building and land you see behind me, which is where the bodies
of Wendell Grimshaw, his wife, and his daughter were found.
Authorities suspect foul play.*

"*Could these murders possibly be related to the five
brutally murdered couples found dead in their home within the
last couple of months? Authorities still have no leads and have
exhausted all options. Will this killer be apprehended or will he
kill again?*

"*I'm Barbara Blalock checking in with the people from
Channel 4 at 6…*"

Mrs. Deveraux watched as the story unfolded in the
news. "The Grimshaw bodies discovered, on my
land…*Tom*. Was this the work of my husband? Could he
be Tom? *He is trying to destroy me.* I have to patch this

up." Mrs. Deveraux knew that the media would be her best line of defense. She jumped into her car and headed to the building site. She had to be sure the media wouldn't leave the scene so she leaked a tip on Channel 4's tip line that she was in the area. Before long, flashing cameras had spotted her gorgeous face. Her seductive unrelenting eyes captured the lens impeccably. She had an undeniable attraction that stopped you in your tracks. For a moment, the world stood silent. Her supremacy and beauty challenged each other for the spotlight. Her sophisticated splendor evoked a pleasant smile from you and her powerful nature cradled you.

She was mesmerizing.

She was lethal.

She was Mrs. Deveraux.

These thoughts ran through the mind of the news crews that congregated at the building site to get a glimpse of the divine Mrs. Deveraux.

"Mrs. Deveraux...do you fear for your life," one of the news reporters abruptly asked.

"Yes, I do. Several of my acquaintances have been murdered. Of course, I fear for my life. I just wish I knew what this was all about."

"Do you have any idea why this building site was targeted or why your acquaintances were killed?" another reported asked.

"No, I do not. My dear, I wish I knew." And with that, she walked away while reporters chased her for more answers. She sat in her vehicle, gazed at the stirring wheel in dismay and pulled off.

Of course, Captain Crawford and Det. Bridges figured this was part of her manipulation. She had to paint herself as a victim, Bridges stated. The Captain agreed but he knew it would work. The media ate it up. Who could resist her charming face, the Captain thought?

Meanwhile, on her way back to Bloomfield Hills, Mrs. Deveraux received a call from Mr. Mullens.

"I found out more information about your husband. You would be pleased to know that the authorities in London dismissed him as a suspect in your mother's case because he had an air tight alibi. The only reason he was questioned was because he delivered milk in the neighborhood."

Mrs. Deveraux was silent.

"Hello, Mrs. Deveraux?"

"Go on…"

"The hospital stay was a little tricky but after extensive research and pulling teeth, I finally got an old surgeon to admit why Mr. Deveraux was in an mental hospital—"

Intrigued set in and she cut Mr. Mullens off, "Why?"

"Your husband had been beaten near death. His face had been beaten unrecognizable; most of his bones in his body had been crushed or fractured; and he had been stabbed nineteen times. This doctor found him in an alley; took him back to the mental hospital where he figured Gericault, well Clayton, would be safe. The doctor performed several surgeries to make him well again.

"The doctor that I spoke to was a little creepy but he explained that it was the *art of the surgery* that drew his interest. He didn't know if he could save Clayton but he felt compelled to try. And after he started to recover from his injuries, the doctor decided to manipulate Clayton's face into something else. He helped him change his identity and flee the country."

Mrs. Deveraux remained silent. She gazed out of the windshield in a daze just as she had stared at the stirring wheel before she left the building site. Her thoughts were unhurried and her moment of clarity had vanished. She was at a lost. She had killed the man she loved based on suspicions. She finally parted her lips to make a statement but she didn't remember speaking, "Go on…"

"It seemed that your husband had come under scrutiny which led to his assault and it was suspected that he fled the country to save his life," Mr. Mullens added.

"What was his air tight alibi?"

"His alibi…" Mr. Mullens shuffled through his papers and replied, "Here it is…he had a childhood injury that caused him to have slow mobility in his right arm. I believe it was some sort of brain injury—I didn't get the specifics."

"That is why he had trouble lifting his right arm over his head. I use to tease him about that," she softly stated.

"I guess…" Mr. Mullens started to feel on edge with Mrs. Deveraux. He couldn't wait until this case was over. Had it not been for the large sum of cash she had paid him, he would have dropped this case like a hot skillet. So, he ignored her frequent pauses and her delayed responses and continued, "I believe this Tom guy may be in bed with a Congressman. Congressman Jerry Phelps, I believe his name is."

"Congressman Phelps?"

"I have to double check this information but I am close to finding out who Tom is and who he is connected to. I am still trying to piece together the significance of the interest in your building and land."

"Please, keep me posted."

Click.

"Phelps, you dirty bastard. What are you up to? You and Senator Joy. If you son-of-a-bitches cross me, I will pin your asses to the cross," Mrs. Deveraux whispered to herself.

THE GRIMSHAW ESTATE was an eerie morbid mansion that was well passed its use by date; primarily because of the lifeless heady scent and the monstrous cobwebs that swarmed you as you entered the wide double doors. The fine threads spun with you while you walked through the mansion. But the very delicateness of the spun webs was somehow mysterious. The feeling of animate weighed heavily on you, even though there were no signs of life. Especially for Bridges who had an unpleasant and confound, yet alluring sense that she had visited this mansion before.

Bridges and Det. Jarrod kept a steady pace while the CSIs raked through the mansion for any possible evidence of Mr. Grimshaw's murder. Miraculously Bridges stumbled upon Mr. Grimshaw's study. "How do I always manage to find the damn studies," she asked herself. Bridges shook her head and proceeded inside the subtly dark and murky room. The Grimshaw study resembled all the other studies from the other crime scenes.

As you enter the study, there's an oversized executive desk as your focal point in the room. An exclusive set of paintings hung systematically across the wall behind the desk. A very distinguishing selection of antique books lay orderly across the built-in shelves on the wall to the left of the office entrance. On the right side: another neat row of books—some not as intriguing—and an intimate ill-light section that housed a cozy plush leather chair and a small handcrafted marble top table with a slim unique table lamp. Bridges smirked when she searched around the room. "Rich people must think alike. Why are all their studies the same? I practically know my way around this office as if I've been here before."

Bridges' self-indulgent chatter came to a screeching halt when her fingers landed on the face of some very interesting documents. In an old unique antique chest, about the size of a one drawer file cabinet, Bridges found old property deeds, a will, and other yellowish papers with faded writing. She could only assume that the faded information on the yellowish documents were just as important as the visible documents she was now scanning. She couldn't believe her eyes.

After Bridges finished at the mansion, she returned to the station, headed down to archives and frantically scoured the records in search of a witness to the information she retrieved from the Grimshaw mansion. Her fingers couldn't move fast enough. She was drawn to the documents in her hand while the uncontrolled steam penetrated her nose.

There it was; the document she had been searching for. It was deeply entrenched in the heart of the vast pile of papers she accumulated during her exploration. "Thomas Grimshaw," she softly said aloud. Bridges knew this case had planted a *personal* stem inside her and now she felt forced to find out who planted the seed.

After her mother's death, Bridges investigated her mother's past to find out where her inheritance originated. She had been well into her investigation when she suddenly felt the urge to let it go. Now, she wished she had continued the search. She knew there was an unnerving feeling that possessed her body when she entered the Grimshaw mansion. It was one she had before, as a child. And it wasn't because the mansion was old, uninhabited, crawling with creepy critters, and it contained an emptiness that overpowered your senses; it was because she had been there before. She had played there before. She had stayed there before. Now...she remembered.

She remembered Thomas too. Her cousin.

Wendell Thomas Grimshaw III was Bridges' great grandfather.

"That's where my mother's inheritance came from. *That twenty-four-million-dollar trust fund she left me.* But why would he leave so much money to her? My mother was an in-law. This doesn't make any sense," she contemplated aloud.

"Where is Thomas now? I have to find him," she barked.

Chapter 19

Inside the Life of a Killer

GRANDFATHER WAS MEAN, THE LITTLE BOY thought. The boy hadn't realized how mean and frightening Grandfather would get until the boy finally woke up from an induced coma. Grandfather was never a gentle and benevolent man. His persona reeked of evil and his aggressive nature was only a hint of his torment.

Mom could never save the little boy. She nurtured the boy and held him a little too close for Grandfather's taste. The little boy's mother remained under Grandfather's spell until her untimely death.

alina

On the day that the little boy's world would unfold, it started out as any other day. His mother had awakened him for breakfast and as the little boy headed down the stairs, he could hear his grandfather's voice roar unmercifully through the massive mansion. At age eleven, the little boy had grown to disregard his grandfather's ranting and raving. It was no secret that Grandfather despised the little boy. Grandfather would proclaim that daily.

It took only a few minutes before the little boy reached the dining hall area but that was too long for grandfather.

"So are we supposed to wait all morning for you?" Grandfather asked heatedly.

The little boy gave no response.

"Answer me when I speak." Grandfather hissed once more.

With his chin hovering over his chest, eyes glued to floor, the little boy responded, "It didn't take me very long."

"Look at me while you speak. You don't even have the decency or the strength to look someone in the eye when you speak to them. You are a weak, pathetic little wimp of a kid and you don't deserve to eat breakfast in this house.

"Now, go back to your room and don't come out until you can accrue some nerve."

"*Father.* You don't have to be so vulgar," the little boy's mother said.

Without warning, Grandfather hammered his fist on the dining table and said, "*Shut up! You don't get to speak anymore young lady; and don't you ever question my orders again!*"

The little boy's mother moved across the room to comfort her child. She guided his direction from the dining hall to the foot of the spiral staircase and secretly whispered, "Go upstairs now baby and momma will bring you something to eat later. Ok? Go baby, please just go."

"What the hell is going on in here?" Grandfather asked angrily.

"Nothing father, just go and eat your breakfast," the little boy's mother said nervously.

"You two think I am a fool. I have manipulated and entangled some of the greatest minds in this business and you think that you can pull the wool over my eyes." The little boy's mother looked up at her father with intense eyes and a knot tightened in the pit of her belly. She knew she couldn't save her child from the horror that was to come.

Out of nowhere, Grandfather shoved the little boy's mother to the side, and with mad force, he extended his enormous arm high in the air and lowered his monstrous hand across the little boy's face. The little boy's body went down quickly. As his fragile body hit the marble floor, his head landed stridently on the sharp edge of the second stair.

No movement.

The little boy's mother gasped, held her hands tightly to her chest and stood in total fright. The little boy lay on the floor, blood slowly spilling from underneath his head while urine crawled across the floor from under his pants.

Still, no movement. The mother watched her baby's life slip away, while the grandfather barked, "Look at what we have here. I told you he was a wimpy, pathetic little boy…he has pissed himself. Get that little shit out of my foyer."

In a small window of three minutes; the little boy was struck, dropped to the floor with massive force, and on his way to the hospital clinging to life. Had it not been for his grandmother, the little boy probably would have died at the bottom of the staircase. The little boy's mother remained in a zombie-like state and said little to the doctors and nurses that attended to her child.

"Ma'am, are you ok? Can you tell me what happened to him?" a heavy nurse, with labored breathing asked, as she sat behind the nurse's station desk sighing in frustration because the little boy's mother hadn't responded to any of their questions for over thirty minutes.

The mother glanced over at the flood of doctors and nurses behind a partially closed curtain, dexterously handling her child as they tried to stop the bleeding. The mother unhurriedly moved her head to face the heavy nurse again and said, "Is my child going to be alright?"

The heavy nurse stared into the woman's empty tenebrous eyes and the glossy glow that hovered around her pupils appeared maroon or a reddish color. Her eyes had the look of a bloody evil that lurked within. The woman's slight teary eye and dilated pupils, masked a complicated hidden secret that could have a profound impact on the only world she has ever known. The nurse thought the woman was on drugs but if she had only known the truth, she couldn't possibly expect her to answer such questions like: *"how did this happen…where you were when this incident occurred…are you aware of the seriousness of this situation?"* the mother thought.

After a while, the mother made her way to the hospital waiting room. The long hours were antagonizing. Shock penetrated her muscles, while the fire continued to burn in her eyes. The thought of losing her child invoked an unsettling force of violent rage that whipped through her body like howling wind. She was no longer chained by the restraints of fear. The echoes of terror had been curbed since witnessing her child's sudden brush with death. The little boy's mother had instantly realized that she was a mother who had an unimpaired need to protect her *son.*

At last, in an imperceptible amble, the handsome clean-cut doctor entered the waiting room, eyes scanning the area for the little boy's mother. He hadn't practiced the words he would say to her but there were no easy words that would describe the complexity of her son's condition.

The handsome doctor walked up to the seemingly fragile woman. He absorbed the eerie sense that was deeply inscribed into the mother's face. A haze rested in her luring eyes and an evil craving manifested inside her. Uncritical, nor haunted by the discomforting pale face mother, the doctor introduced himself, shook her hand, and started his spill.

"We administered several test to determine if your son sustained any internal damage from his fall and a CAT scan showed that he has an intracranial hemorrhage which is bleeding in the brain. Of course, our primary goal was to stop the bleeding or at least relieve the pressure that was building inside the brain preventing the flow of oxygen. Your son has lapsed into a coma because of this interruption of oxygen and the head trauma.

"We had to phone our pediatric neurosurgeon to perform an emergency brain surgery to prevent further damage. We were finally able to relieve some of the pressure but we had to remove parts of his left frontal lobe." The doctor paused for a fleeting moment, and then he continued once he examined the unhinged facial expression of the woman. It was almost as if she was waiting for the floor to drop; but the inescapable fact was that she was waiting for the doctor to tell her that her *son* would not live much longer.

"We also ran a few other tests to determine his hemoglobin levels because your son lost a lot of blood, too much blood in relation to the type of cut he sustained on his forehead. And we had a very difficult time controlling his bleeding during the surgery. There was so much blood lost, at one point we thought we were going to lose him. Frankly, it's truly a miracle that he's still alive and holding on. Were you aware that your son has a bleeding disorder?

"Of course, we will have to run more conclusive tests to be certain but it appears that your son may have *Hemophilia*, which is a rare bleeding disorder that prevents the blood from clotting normally. This would explain the massive head injury, the profuse bleeding, and other bruises that mirror child abuse."

The little boy's mother finally glanced over for a subtle peek of the doctor and responded, "No, I didn't know he had a bleeding disorder. Is that dangerous?" Realizing that she had asked a question that could only be answered with a look of, *are you serious*, written across the doctor's face; the woman cleared her throat and tried to rephrase her obvious question.

However, before she could mutter another foolish word, the doctor politely responded as if she had asked a thoughtful intriguing question, "Yes, bleeding disorders are very serious. In fact, his hemophilia would prevent him from having a full recovery. Still, it is too early to tell but the procedure went well and we are hopeful that he will awake from his coma soon. It is still touch and go at this point, but we are still hopeful. Although it is very likely that he will have long-term complications, with many treatment options available, your son should live a more productive life than you may anticipate."

"What treatment options?"

"The treatment for *hemophilia* is typically recombinant plasma, a *Factor VIII Replacement Therapy* medication."

LITTLE DID THE doctors know, the little boy's head injury had destroyed a child and a killer was born. The boy suffered damaged to his frontal and temporal lobes which helped create his violent and aggressive behavior. The boy's mother had suffered damage too and the evil that manifested inside her had unfolded in a methodical hunt for revenge.

Chapter 20

Fancy Meeting a Killer Here

I N PURSUIT OF A KILLER, BRIDGES DECIDED TO follow Sgt. Willowbee. Bridges sat in her police cruiser still taken aback from Sgt. Willowbee's behavior at the Kensington crime scene. She waited edgily for Sgt. Willowbee to exit the station. She made sure she parked two rows back from Sgt. Willowbee's police car so he wouldn't see her. She narrowed her eyes intricately, mentally studying all the information her brain had absorbed about the killings. There were many times where she thought she had reached the moment of clarity, until she was hit with another bizarre blow.

She thought of the gruesome murders, the FBI's involvement, the suspicious behavior of her superiors, the peculiar unique evidence that the forensic lab had analyzed, and the fact that Mrs. Deveraux came full circle around all of this. "This case is too complicated. There must have been years of planning and waiting. Perhaps this is why the killer has been able to elude us; *he is one of us*, she thought. Bridges had trouble swallowing this possibility.

"There he is." she said excitingly. She pulled her wheels from the parking spot to follow Sgt. Willowbee. She wanted to speed up behind him to let him know she was following him because she didn't care. She wanted him to know. But she knew she wouldn't get anywhere with that kind of stunt. So, she kept a safe distance and followed him along a familiar path.

Minutes later, Sgt. Willowbee pulled his police cruiser to the curb of a familiar building. It was the offices of Julie Ann Deveraux. Bridges watched from a distance as Sgt. Willowbee stretched his body across the passenger seat as if he was looking for something in the glove box. From her distance, she couldn't tell what he was reaching for. Moments later, his head resurfaced, he glanced out the driver side window, turned back to face the front windshield and Bridges noticed he had his cell phone pressed against his ear.

A tall built man, handsomely dressed with a detective swag, exits the building and got into a black sedan that was parked several feet from Sgt. Willowbee's police cruiser. Bridges had never seen him before. She remembered that Mrs. Deveraux indicated she would conduct her own investigation so Bridges figured he must be the P.I.

As soon as the black sedan pulled from the curb, Sgt. Willowbee pulled his police car from the curb to follow.

"Is he following the P.I.," Bridges asked aloud, pulling her police cruiser from the curb to follow as well. "I see no one can be trusted around here," she said disdainfully.

Bridges following Sgt. Willowbee, who followed the P.I. and they stopped at another familiar place but no one exited their vehicles, *why*, she thought. Shortly after all vehicles were stopped, a slender man exit the front door of a familiar house. "I know I know this place. I've seen this place somewhere before," Bridges whispered to herself.

The slender man jumped into a Mercedes Benz and drove off. The black sedan followed a few moments after the slender man took off and Sgt. Willowbee pulled off moments later.

"What are they up to," Bridges asked herself. "Are all three of these men involved?"

It was getting too complicated and Bridges thought she would be caught. She contemplated what she should do but before she could make a decision, fifteen minutes later, they arrived at another house. The slender man got out of his vehicle, the P.I. pulled out a camera, and Sgt. Willowbee slowly drove by. Bridges had to make a split second decision, "Do I follow the sergeant or do I stay and find out who these men are?"

Bridges leaned over the passenger seat and quickly scrambled through her glove box for a pen to write down the address and plate number of the P.I. She had to be sure he was the private investigator that Mrs. Deveraux hired.

After writing down the address, she took off to catch up with Sgt. Willowbee. Her tires slightly squealed and as she drove by, the P.I. removed his camera from his face and peeked back at Bridges.

Her heart pound from the adrenaline and she had hoped that the man in the black sedan didn't get a good look at her, just in case he was the killer or the killer's accomplice.

She finally caught up to Sgt. Willowbee and in a flash, she had to step on her brakes, just missing a truck moving cross traffic because she hadn't noticed the red light on her side of the traffic signal. The front of Bridges police car nosedived toward the pavement while the back of the car fearlessly bounce up and down as the car slightly veered to the right.

Bridges' head thrust forward toward the windshield but her seatbelt disrupted the flow. Minor aches clouded her head; blurred vision clouded her eyes, and an agonizing sting attacked her left shoulder. "*Dammit,*" she said aloud while trying to resist the immediate confusion. She shook her head several times and as soon as the light turned she peeled off. She had lost Sgt. Willowbee but she had a hunch.

"I was right, there he is," Bridges confirmed to herself. "So he is working for Mrs. Deveraux." Bridges took a glimpse out her car window as she slowly drove by and spotted Sgt. Willowbee's police cruiser parked in front of Mrs. Deveraux's office building again.

Bridges glanced at the address she scribbled on a loose piece of paper in the car, "I gotta find out who lives at this address. They could be the next victims." She quickly pulled off and after two blocks; she turned on her sirens to bypass any other traffic lights.

BRIDGES REALIZED THAT she had to find the unknown male donor of the blood sample that was extracted from the paintings left at each crime scene. She thought, perhaps, one of these leads would pan out as she entered the address and license plate number into the system, hoping for a viable hit.

After the FBI laboratory performed an extensive analysis of the blood evidence, Bridges learned that the unknown male donor had a rare bleeding disorder and he would need a special recombinant plasma drug called *Factor VIII* to survive any injuries or bleeding episodes. Armed with this information, Bridges started her search.

She researched more information on *hemophilia*, which wasn't much, and she wanted to see if she could locate a patient that may be receiving this type of medication. No hits so far.

Bridges also learned that the other blood found within the paintings were part of a Lot. of blood that went missing in 1982 from a blood bank that has been closed for over twelve years. Bridges discovered that this particular Lot of blood work was set to be destroyed because it was contaminated with hepatitis and HIV which affected hundreds of children with *hemophilia* during that decade.

After the fifth painting was discovered at the Kensington crime scene, authorities knew the killer had to have left the paintings. And as each painting was examined extensively, it was determined that the blood contributors were from the unknown male, the previous murdered victims, and more donors from the Lot of blood from the 80s blood bank.

Bridges was determined to find the unknown male donor. "He's our killer," she whispered to herself.

Chapter 21

Mr. Mullens is on the Case

M R. MULLENS DREADED CALLING MRS. Deveraux. Her behavior had gotten more bizarre with each passing day, he thought. He knew this information would be the icing on the cake and his investigation would be concluded. He took an immense breath and exhaled noisily. He cleared his throat and held the phone loosely to his right ear.

"Mrs. Deveraux...I found Tom," he said with much engagement.

"Who the hell is he?" she asked abruptly.

"His real name is Anthony Garraty. He is the husband of Heather Smits, Ronald Smits's daughter."

"What? Ronald Smits's daughter? Well, well, well…look which way the wind is blowing," Mrs. Deveraux replied. You could see her pleasing smile through the phone.

"I believe our friend got acquainted with Smits when he was Reginald Hensley."

"I don't follow…"

"Smits changed his name to Reginald Hensley, and then he got into a sticky situation down in Florida that forced him to come back to his old heritage. So, Smits ditched the name *Reginald Hensley* and changed it back to Ronald Smits. It appeared to be some kind of rebellious fling."

"What kind of trouble?" Mrs. Deveraux asked with curiosity.

"He was the primary suspect in a brutal murder of a couple and the case was relatively similar to the killings here. The police have already looked into these coincidences and turned up nothing," Mr. Mullens replied.

"But how does Mr. Garraty play into Mr. Smits life?"

"I haven't figured that out yet but Garraty may have used Smits for info."

"Interesting…"

"It looks like our friend was a busy little boy. I found pictures of you, your partners (including the deceased victims), Senator Joy and Congressman Phelps plastered across a cork board. I also found documents..."

"Documents? What documents?" she asked hurriedly.

"Quitclaim deeds, information of forgery, and what looked to be commercial real estate transfers of some sort. I am sure you may be able to make it out. I'm afraid it's all Greek to me," Mr. Mullens jokily said. He laughed briefly and continued, "It appeared that Mr. Garraty had been watching you for some time, perhaps years. He had some of the same information that I had obtained on your husband. He is incredibly meticulous Mrs. Deveraux; I don't think we need to underestimate this guy. He is very clever and resourceful. I'm still trying to find the source of his finances."

"Trust me; I have learned to never underestimate my opponent."

"I can't quite understand why, but Mr. Garraty had information on Senator Joy and Congressman Phelps as it related to your building site."

"What do you mean?"

"Scanning through the paperwork, it looked as if Senator Joy didn't share the same vision as you. The paperwork suggests (based on Mr. Garraty's findings) that Senator Joy and Congressman Phelps were trying to postpone your project."

"*Why would they care? There has got to be another angle that I am missing here,*" she said furiously.

"I was thinking the same thing so I dug a little deeper into Senator Joy's background. My resources would take a little longer to retrieve any in-tell on Phelps; but my sources say that Senator Joy was trying to get money out of Congress for the state budget. He wanted the government to declare the state destitute and he petitioned for emergency funding for welfare, Medicaid, and community outsourcing programs designed to help individuals who are unemployed, etc. There was a Fund created that housed the proceeds received for these programs but the Fund is assumed to be fictitious.

"However, my sources also told me that Senator Joy was '*unofficially*' investigated in the past for using federal and state funding for his own personal gain. He had many venture capital investments that he couldn't validate as legitimate government investments. I also obtained rumored information that Senator Joy is harboring a dark secret. It turns out that the disgusting bastard may be into little boys but I couldn't get anyone to confirm or deny these allegations.

"This guy is something else. I also entertained the idea that Mr. Garraty may be getting his finances from Senator Joy and Phelps. This may explain why he was able to retrieve so much information about you and tap into some of the same influential circles as yours."

"But why would my building be of interest to either of them?"

"My guess is that your development would constitute growth, advancement, or progress. If your project was successful, it would mean that the state had its own chance of recovery from the recession – *without the help of congress.*

"Your project would pose a threat to Senator Joy's cash cow funding source," Mr. Mullens examined.

"So how does Mr. Garraty play a role in this? Why would he be helping Senator Joy and Phelps?"

"Now you are asking the curious questions I wanted to know the answers to."

"Ronald was not a political man, he was a religious man. So why is Ronald Smits's son-in-law wrapped up into political warfare?"

Mr. Mullens remained silent.

"There has got to be a personal connection for Mr. Garraty," Mrs. Deveraux added. "Did you find any other information about Mr. Garraty?"

"I did some checking and Mr. Garraty's existence is a mystery before 1994. I could only assume that Anthony Garraty is a new identity," Mr. Mullens stated matter-of-factly.

"What would he be hiding from?" Mrs. Deveraux couldn't sharply distinguish the reasoning behind Mr. Garraty's active or inactive existence. One could only speculate that Mr. Garraty had interest in the building and land but of a taller order. "Mr. Grimshaw," she cried out.

"Mr. Grimshaw? *Wendell Grimshaw*...the body that was recovered a few days ago?" Mr. Mullens asked inquisitively.

"Yes, that's it Mr. Mullens. Anthony Garraty must be somehow related to Mr. Grimshaw," she said with uninhibited certainty.

"But how can you be so sure?"

"It's the only thing that fits. There had to be something more than the incentive of money to drive a man to enter a crude world of uncertainty. He said he wanted me to suffer just as he had suffered. In his twisted psychotic brain, he truly believes that I have taken everything from him, even though the bane of his existence had been a mystery, even to me."

"I thought your lawyers took care of that. I thought they determined that Mr. Grimshaw had no living relatives or at least no living relative came forward to claim the estate," he recalled.

"Yes, you are correct. No one stepped forward to claim the estate. I suppose the inextricable relationship that Mr. Garraty had with Mr. Grimshaw caused enough damage for him to stay away from Bloomfield Hills." Mrs. Deveraux paused for a moment and continued, "Now, the devil has come to collect on his promise." A concrete expression sterilized her face and Mrs. Deveraux found herself wandering off again, "I saw him, you know."

"You saw who..."

"The Devil. He was in my dream and he wanted my soul," she softly stated.

"What are you talking about Mrs. Deveraux?"

"I thought my husband was the Devil and he set out to destroy me."

"What do you mean, Mrs. Deveraux?"

"I erased him…"

"Who?"

"Clayton."

"Why?"

"I thought he was *Tom*," Mrs. Deveraux exclaimed.

She shook her head, took in a deep breath and cunningly laughed, "Don't worry dear, I am simply mumbling."

Mr. Mullens wasn't sure if he should be turning Mrs. Deveraux in to the authorities or the mental institution. Nevertheless, he realized she was breaking…*and fast.*

"I will get to the bottom of Senator Joy's and Phelps involvement. Don't you worry about them," Mrs. Deveraux insisted.

"No problem. Please, be my guest."

"You have outdone yourself Mr. Mullens. You found Tom."

Mr. Mullens smiled arrogantly and said, "I will bring the documents to you that I retrieved from Mr. Garraty's place of residence and the photos I took of him, tomorrow at six pm."

"That would be fine Mr. Mullens. Thank you."

A sentiment he hadn't expected, *thank you*. But he did however, anticipate Mrs. Deveraux end the call without saying goodbye.

Mrs. Deveraux knew Mr. Mullens findings were correct about Senator Joy. The Senator had been harboring a deep concealed secret and until now, Mrs. Deveraux was the only one who knew about it—*for sure*. Mrs. Deveraux knew *all* his secrets: His faulty Fund, his sickening fetish with little boys, and his unscrupulous politics. It was the Senator who helped Mrs. Deveraux acquire the Grimshaw Estate in such a short time and with little paperwork. He was willing to do anything to hush his little secrets and he knew she would make his life a living hell.

Mrs. Deveraux deliberated on the information that Mr. Mullens just shared with her and determined that Senator Joy and Congressman Phelps were the driving force behind this horrific situation. She knew this day would come and she had thought she would be prepared to do whatever necessary to handle it. With all her spiteful acts of greed and deceit, she knew it would be time for this evil spirit to come to collect and she felt Senator Joy was the man to do it. He was trying to destroy her and perhaps have Tom kill her. Only, she couldn't figure out why Tom. Why would he want to kill her business partners, especially in such a bizarre and horrific manner? It just didn't make sense. "Unless, they are trying to destroy me by making me a prime suspect in these murders…that would be a way to do it," she profoundly claimed.

Then she recalled that Mr. Mullens indicated that her project meant growth and development. "They are trying to hinder my project. Is that why these last court proceedings seem to be dragging along? *I must put a stop to this madness at once.*"

Chapter 22

Closing in on a Psychopath

RIDGES DETERMINED THAT THE SLENDER MAN was Anthony Garraty, the husband of Heather Smits-Garraty. *"Ronald Smits's daughter!"* Bridges glanced at the computer screen and added, "I knew these murders revolved around that first crime scene, *I was right*." She gazed into the screen again and jumped from her desk chair, "I have to tell the Captain."

Bridges vigorously searched for Captain Crawford but he was nowhere to be found. The dryness in her mouth had taken over her and she knew she was on to something. She frantically rubbed her fingers over her mouth, pondering a plan. Bridges bit down on her lip, just as she had always done when faced with an intense decision. She knew she needed to trail Mr. Garraty, but she also needed to trail Mrs. Deveraux and somehow Sgt. Willowbee had to be followed. She needed help but she didn't know who to trust.

Before she could mull over this situation any further, the station clerk brought over a package for Bridges. It was Thomas Grimshaw's belongings from the European Art Institute. After examining the contents, Bridges' decision had been made for her.

She would follow Garraty. Bridges followed Garraty to Mrs. Deveraux's building site off Lasher Road. Security was posted so he had to enter through another way. He traveled along a quaint side street, got out of a black SUV, and entered through a broken section of the fence.

"What is so damn important about this site? What is he looking for?" Bridges said aloud. She sat in her police cruiser and watched through a pair of small binoculars. After Garraty had disappeared from her immediate view, she bit her lip, rubbed her thumb against the fingers on her left hand and made the decision to follow him.

She bolted across the side street from where she had parked and ran to follow in Garraty's footsteps. She approached the gate, scanned her surroundings, and crawled through the opening. As she tried to straighten her body, she realized her pants leg was caught on a sharp part of the broken fence. She tugged and tugged and lost her balance. Her left elbow hit the gravel, hard. She anxiously looked up and turned her head from left to right. She practically injured her neck when she looked behind her to trace a subtle noise.

With her body facing the gate, she swiftly struggled to unhook her pants. She hadn't seen the dark shadow that larked behind her.

"Hello, Det. Bridges," a voice from the darkness cried out.

Bridges head snapped back in sudden fright. She froze. She no longer concentrated on her pants entwined in the gate. She no longer had a thought of why Garraty was at this building site. This unexpected burst of dialogue had frozen her thoughts completely.

"Why are you following me Detective?" the voice asked. Bridges could hear him moving closer. She snapped out of her unsettling coma and realized that the voice was Garraty.

"Why are you here?" she finally managed to say.

"Ahh, ahh, my question first Detective," he said smoothly.

"I was following you," she replied cautiously.

"*Why*...I said?" he said with a pale hint of enmity.

"You're Anthony Garraty, right."

"What's it to you Detective? What have you been up to Lady?" Garraty's smiling face came into view. He took slow steps toward Bridges. She eagerly searched his body to see if he had a gun or a weapon. Nothing. However, his right hand was curled as if he had a small object inside.

As Garraty moved in closer, Bridges could see the resemblance. "Your real name is Thomas Grimshaw." she blurted out.

His footsteps paused. Complexity was smeared across his face and his eyelids blinked rapidly. "What name did you call me?"

Bridges could feel the tension mounting and she had not figured out her next move, so she decided to keep him talking. "I remember you, Thomas. Don't you remember me?"

"Of course, I know you; you're that detective that is investigating those murders," he said matter-of-factly.

"I know you from years before," she assured.

"What do you mean?"

"I use to play with you when we were younger." Bridges slowly tried to pull her trapped leg from the fence and keep Garraty talking, hoping he would reveal some vital information.

He remained silent.

Bridges continued her questions, hoping one would be answered soon, "Why did you change your name and where have you been all this time?"

"I've been around. Why are you asking so many questions?" he said, losing patience.

"I'm sorry. I just thought we could catch-up. You know…we're cousins."

"Cousins? But…how…why?"

"My mother is related to your grandfather—"

He briskly interrupts, *"Don't speak of him. He's nothing to me."*

"Ok, ok, I won't mention his name again. But you have got to help me Thomas. I seem to be tangled here," she managed a weird laugh and pointed to her trapped pants leg.

"Why should I help you? You never told me why you were here and why you were following me?"

"I thought I could talk to you Thomas. I was trying to find an heir to Mr. Grimshaw's estate because I didn't want Mrs. Deveraux to get her greedy little hands on it and I found you." Bridges took a chance mentioning his grandfather's name again. She especially monitored his reaction when she mentioned Mrs. Deveraux.

"Yes, Mrs. Deveraux, the greediest woman I know. I don't want Mr. Grimshaw's estate, she can have it."

"Then why are you here? Why are you on Mrs. Deveraux's property, especially where your grandfather and mother's body was found?" Bridges was tired of playing. Even though she lay on the ground, vulnerable, she could no longer hold her tongue.

"Pretty bold questions for someone with their head in the gravel," Garraty calmly pointed out.

After Bridges panic had subsided and her ego and anger took hold of her, she quickly unraveled her pants leg and swiftly jumped to her feet.

Garraty didn't budge. His psychosis warrants him the inability to be startled and a high tolerance for fear. He gave Bridges a blank stare, and then all of a sudden, he swung his right arm and landed a mighty blow to Bridges' left shoulder. Before she could react, she felt her legs weaken and then she collapsed.

"You really should have stayed out of my business Det. Bridges." Garraty kneeled down to scan Bridges paralyzed body. He knew the injection would wear off within a few hours and he debated if he wanted to leave her alive.

There was a small shed to the rear of the building site, next to the broken fence opening that Bridges and Garraty crawled through; Garraty decided to place her body inside. He didn't want to create a disturbance, so he searched for a heavy object to bash her head in.

"It would be morning before they realize she is here and by that time, I would have completed my masterpiece."

Chapter 23

On a Wild Goose Chase

"MRS. DEVERAUX, I HAVE TO ASK, ARE YOU involved in these murders?"

"Interpretation of the evidence can swing in many directions Mr. Mullens. I feel I must be appalled by your accusations." She smiles and pours a drink of dark liquor. The dark liquid had been placed inside the fancy bottle many, many months ago; she had no idea what she was about to digest. She was really more concerned with the bull she had to digest from Mr. Mullens.

"It appears that you and Senator Joy was in-bed together on several questionable deals: the Grimshaw Estate transaction, fraudulent documents or forged documents, suspicion of murder. I have to ask, are you involved?"

"Although sometimes I enjoy entertaining bull Mr. Mullens, I have no intensions on entertaining you today so please leave your questions to a minimum and note that your investigation has concluded," she said angelically, while taking a sip of the dark liquor.

"You still have not answered my question, Mrs. Deveraux," he repeated. He was running out of patience and demanded answers.

"And I don't plan to Mr. Mullens. I will not entertain this foolishness," she said with certainty.

"Then you leave me no choice."

"We always have a choice Mr. Mullens and you just made one," she replied ferociously. She delicately turned her head and glanced over her left shoulder at Mr. Mullens. He had seen that look before. It was the undeniable look of a killer.

Mrs. Deveraux's fierce trait unraveled from the mighty blow. Her hair delicately hung over her left eye and fragments were inhaled by her open mouth. She had stunned herself. She studied over Mr. Mullens's collapsed body. Before she could gnaw on the scene any further; in walks Tom.

Clap, clap, clap.

"I knew you had it in you, Mrs. Deveraux."

Her body jerked from the bombshell and she took two steps backward, moving away from Tom in unremarkable fear. She hadn't construed Tom to be a man of many talents or guts. She hadn't anticipated his visit tonight. She didn't respond.

"Why didn't you use your pistol that you have tucked away in your nightstand drawer?" he said with a smirk.

"How did you…"

"Oh, I've been here before Mrs. Deveraux." He smiled candidly and continued, "I know all your little secrets. I could have killed you a few months ago, but I wanted you to suffer, just as I had suffered."

"Why would your suffering matter to me? I don't owe you anything Mr. Tom," she stated with sarcasm, trying to hide her bafflement.

"You still have to try and be in charge, *hum* Mrs. Deveraux," he replied. Then he pulled his pistol from the back waist of his pants. As Mr. Mullens lay bleeding on the floor, Tom aimed the pistol at Mr. Mullens' head and pulled the trigger.

The echoed ringing noise from the blast violently penetrated Mrs. Deveraux's ears. She bent over as if she would vomit and covered her ears aggressively. She collapsed her eyelids for a transitory moment, regained her posture, and quickly refocused her eyes on Tom.

"See...that is how you would do that," he said jokingly and smiled. "You look tense Mrs. Deveraux. Why is that?"

"What do you want?" She heavily sighed and her anger started to take form. "I don't owe you *shit*, why are you here."

"Aww, you don't want to play anymore; I'm hurt. Just when I thought you were having fun," Tom said mockingly.

"I suppose now you think you've got me by the balls. Well...I won't have it. I don't care if it is in this life or the next; I will put a knife through your heart young man." Her treacherous words echoed the room, just as the gunshot blast had mastered.

The mystified look on Tom's face confirmed that he had been caught off balance. Tom knew Mrs. Deveraux was cold-hearted but he didn't expect this response. "This lady has got some serious nerve," he murmured to himself.

Tom tried to regain his momentum and announced, "Look lady, I will put a bullet through your head just as I did the others."

"What others?" she quickly asked, trying to keep him talking.

"Smits, Langdon, Holmes...you know what others, don't play *stupid*."

"So you killed them all? But why?" she asked daringly.

"I had no choice—"

Mrs. Deveraux quickly interrupts, "We always have a choice. It's the choice that you make that decides your fate."

"I had to...no...I needed to destroy *you*, Mrs. Deveraux," he said with building anger.

"But I don't understand why. I know that I have stepped on a few toes every now and then but I honestly don't remember you. I wouldn't have forgotten those eyes," she added in her softest voice of persuasion, "I knew that was you when I saw you in court. Your little outburst was touching. Why would you wait so long before striking?"

"I had a plan. You see, killing Ronald was supposed to be the end of Plan A but it didn't turn out that way. Ronald's death should have been concluded as a religious cult killing or something to that effect. Once I had underestimated you and your power, I had to form a Plan B, and believe me, it was challenging. You do drive a hard bargain Mrs. Deveraux." Tom smiled, revealing his gorgeous white teeth. He was a site for sore eyes, Mrs. Deveraux secretly thought. But she knew, if she was going to walk out of this house alive, she had to put all her manipulating charm into overdrive. She was willing to do whatever it took.

"May I," Mrs. Deveraux motioned her hand toward the cream leather sofa and asked if it was ok for her to sit. "You know, I'm not as young these days." She smiled and Tom smiled back. He hadn't formulated a Plan C so he decided to indulge Mrs. Deveraux.

"Please, by all means, have a seat," his sarcastic tone wasn't ignored.

Mrs. Deveraux relaxed her bottom on the plush cushion of the sofa, unhurriedly crossed one leg over the other and released a soft sigh as she rested her back against the sofa. "You still haven't told me why you were after me."

With the gun relaxed at Tom's side, she felt she could take the floor.

"I needed Smits to get close to you and I had to do that through his daughter."

"I see. That explains how you were able to follow my court proceedings. Pretty clever."

"Thank you. That feels like an honor coming from you," he stated and smiled.

Mrs. Deveraux nodded and smiled, ignoring the crude narcissism. *"I still don't understand why everyone was so interested in my affairs. It burns me up to see such meddling."* Her frustrations carried its own conversation through the room. Her piercing tongue sent a lethal gas that field the room like smog. Mrs. Deveraux knew Tom had left out his connection to the Congressman and Senator but she didn't want to push her luck. She decided to simply keep him talking until she devised a plan of her own.

"Because you have everything, Mrs. Deveraux, that is why everyone is in your business. You have everything and yet you are still hungry as if you hadn't eaten in a year. It was hunger that drew me to you. It wasn't as important for the police to discover the bodies at the building site as it became important for me to destroy you at any cost. You were just like my grandfather; you had to have it all. Being rich and wealthy and powerful above your means was not good enough for you, you had to have it all."

"So you killed your grandfather Wendell Grimshaw too?" she asked as politely as she could possibly muster.

"You damn right I did. I beat his face in until there was nothing left to see."

"I saw that…"

Tom almost yanked his body out of his pants. He didn't know what that meant when Mrs. Deveraux indicated that she *saw it*; however, he didn't want Mrs. Deveraux to get a whiff of him detaining the comment. He decided not to respond and he finished revealing his tale. "You have no idea what that man put me through. The betrayal, the abuse, the lies and anger was just the beginning of his monstrous storm. I suffered unmercifully at the hands of my *so-called grandfather Wendell*." Tom softly laughed and added, "You know that son-of-a-bitch put me in a coma once?"

mrs. deveraux

"The people you killed, I was simply their business partners; how does their personal life intertwine with mine?" she asked sincerely.

"As I said, it started out with me trying to get a hold of that damn building and land and after I met you, I saw my grandfather all over again. *You had to be destroyed Mrs. Deveraux, don't you see that*," he confirmed. His wrinkled eyebrows, narrowed eyes, and serious expression held the severe circumstances behind his words. "The game is over Mrs. Deveraux. I am through playing around with you."

Mrs. Deveraux could see that she was losing control, if she ever had any. "Ok, Tom, please, can we just talk for a moment. After all, you are here to kill me so why not let me listen to everything you have ever wanted to say to me or to your grandfather. If your grandfather was anything like me, I'm sure you didn't get to speak as often as you would've liked and it infuriated you...*right*."

Tom seemed puzzled and answered, "He never let me talk. He said I was a disappointment and was marked for doom." Tom collapsed his lean body against the living room wall and his subtle tone mystified Mrs. Deveraux. "He never let me talk. My mother was mean to me too but I always got to talk to her. She sent me away after I had awakened from my coma but I had hoped she would come from me."

Feeling she had a little control in the room, Mrs. Deveraux gradually stood up from the sofa and softly whispered Tom's name. His physique had swelled but his curiosity silenced him. She suddenly realized that she wasn't acting or playing a part, she was in-all of Tom's relentless conniving persona.

She was impressed and intrigued. Her mesmerizing brown eyes had a glare of desire that couldn't be unwritten. Her water filled eyes squinted provocatively. But the intoxication of the adrenaline that seeped through her veins was still unnerving. A sensual smile drifted into place as she started to walk toward Tom. She had to put her mind in survival mode and appeal to the trapped boy inside of Tom. The feelings of terror and hunger and bemusement were saturated across her luminous face. She had met her match.

"Tom." Her flirtatious voice echoed in the air. "I am clearly impressed. You are a man of joyous surprises." Mrs. Deveraux's words rolled off her tongue in a wicked but delicate tone. Tom was equally surprised but not by her shock; he had been captivated by his own frozen reaction as he faintly glanced over Mrs. Deveraux's gorgeous face. He had never been as spellbound for a woman as he had been with Mrs. Deveraux. Her alluring nature was poisonous and he knew this, yet his mind had already started to weaken from her lethal serum.

He heard a desperate plea for his attention and he answered, "Mrs. Deveraux, I am shocked that you are surprised." The curious smile embossed across his face told Mrs. Deveraux that she could proceed with caution.

She relaxed her footsteps for a precarious moment and then continued once her eyes connected with Tom's eyes and she could feel he needed her near. She moved closer and closer, heart pounding in irregular beats, mouth drying from excess inhalation. She took a deep breath and collapsed her exhaled breath on Tom's right cheek. Her breath danced off his cheek, across his ear and penetrated his senses. He almost melted.

"This is not how this was supposed to go Mrs. Deveraux," he said with a frog in his throat. He wanted to destroy Mrs. Deveraux with everything he had but her persona reminded him of his mother. He could destroy the things around her but he collapsed into a little boy again whenever he come near her.

"What happen to Julie Ann?" she softly whispered in his ear.

"Julie Ann," he slowly repeated. "This is not how this should—"

She interrupted his statement by gently placing her lips on top of his. They both closed their eyes. His hands lingered around her slim waist with much uncertainty. She pulled away from the motionless kiss and she looked at him with such curiosity and fragileness. It was then that Mrs. Deveraux realized she had been entangled inside her own web of deceit.

A complex look obtruded across Mrs. Deveraux's face and she suddenly knew what she had to do. "Let's unwind in the bedroom," she surprisingly whispered.

"Let me freshen up a bit. It will only take a millisecond," she said convincingly.

A minute later, she reappeared, standing absorbingly close to Tom. His nose captured a whiff of her enticing aroma. It was unforgettable. He indistinctly whispered, "Mother."

Tom had been overwhelmed by Mrs. Deveraux's charismatic manipulation for one reason and it wasn't for the reason's Mrs. Deveraux had determined.

"I knew you would come for me," he said in a repulse tone.

Mrs. Deveraux jolted away from the close net reverie of her body pressed against his and stared at Tom in bewilderment. Her magnetic eyes narrowed unsteadily and she witnessed her unyielding Knight dwindle away into a little boy.

Tom gasped noisily. His head slowly bent forward while his hand pressed firmly against the left side of his stomach. The pain had intensified with every passing breath.

Tom impulsively stepped back and that's when he saw a sharp instrument protruding from Mrs. Deveraux's hand. Her firm grip confirmed that it was not an accident. Disgust distributed across her face and he could see the malevolence inside her.

"Why would you do this to me *Mother*? I had longed for your return; to feel your touch again. I knew you would come back for me," he chanted in a vaporous whisper. Tom's body collapsed on the bed. He firmly held his side and pleasantly waited for the end. An unexpected beam drifted in place and he knew and felt his mother loved him.

His moment of pleasure was interrupted by Mrs. Deveraux when she said, *"I'm not your mother you blundering idiot."*

Tom looked up at Mrs. Deveraux enraged. As he was so often called a "blundering idiot" by his grandfather. He quickly sprung from the bed and as if he hadn't been deeply wounded, he backhand Mrs. Deveraux sending her body soaring clear across the bedroom. He ran to her like a madman and pulled her by her lengthy hair and dragged her back to the bed. He tossed her body to the floor next to the bed like a rag doll.

Unexpectedly, flashes of his eradicated past emerged and Mrs. Deveraux's body disappeared and Tom frightfully saw his grandfather pinned underneath him. Feeling worthless, as his grandfather had made him feel, infuriated Tom into a rage that would send Mrs. Deveraux's face flying from side to side from the massive blows of his steady fist.

She was nearly knocked unconscious before she could free her right arm and swung it toward his face.

He snapped out of his trance. He looked down at Mrs. Deveraux's bloody face, nearly disfigured from the mighty blows, and a horrified expression engulfed his face and the dismayed feelings for his mother were exhumed.

He gently grabbed Mrs. Deveraux's body from the floor and held her tight as the tears rolled from his eyes. Her face was numb from the pain and her fear had worn off. Pure evil was the only adrenaline that she could muster.

Her eyes were barely visible but she tried to search the room for some sort of weapon that she could put in Tom's heart. She slowly rolled her face to her right side and there it was. The pair of scissors she used to stab Tom in the stomach. She just had to find a way to get to them.

"Tom, please you're hurting me. Please, Tom," Mrs. Deveraux tried to plea for Tom to remove the strong hold he had over her body.

Tom blinked rapidly as if he had been standing in a strange place. His reality had faltered. His sense of wrong and right had vanished. Tom removed his body from Mrs. Deveraux's chest tenderly. He hadn't taken notice of his interminable pain. And in his softest voice, he said, "I'm sorry mother. I didn't mean to kill you. I didn't want to but I had to."

Mrs. Deveraux decided to play into Tom's hand. "What are you sorry about dear?" she said groggily. Her mind under like a spell from the pounding trauma to the head.

"I'm sorry I had to kill you and grandfather. He was always so mean. He was very mean. He hurt me mother, just as you have…but I forgave you *mother*. You were always everything to me." He continued to speak but it was apparent that his loss of blood was too much for Tom. His bleeding disorder aided in his quick death.

As Tom leaned against the bed and rested his eyes, Mrs. Deveraux gradually inched across the floor, grinding her fingers deep inside the carpet in search for the scissors. She grabbed hold of the scissors and made her way back to the side of the bed where Tom sat. She didn't know if she had the strength to insert the sharp instrument but pure evil forced her hand.

Abruptly, she plunged the scissors directly in the middle of Tom's chest. He didn't flinch, his stance didn't alter. He welcomed the heart piercing object and watched as Mrs. Deveraux inserted and removed the scissors. The blood poured from his chest and Tom was finally no more.

MRS. DEVERAUX FELL to the floor with useless energy. "It has been a long time since I felt powerless," she muttered to herself and laughed. All of a sudden she couldn't stop laughing. An uncontrollable urge to laugh hysterically hit her like a freight train. She couldn't stop…until she finally passed out.

Chapter 24

Over My Dead Body

"WHERE THE HELL IS BRIDGES?" CAPTAIN Crawford yelled through his opened office door, demanding an answer.

"Captain, I think she was on to something big. There is a package on her desk and her computer has an address of Anthony Garraty. I pulled Garraty's drivers licenses and it resembles a..." Det. Jarrod pulled out his pocket size black notepad and worriedly continued, "...a Thomas Grimshaw."

"Grimshaw?"

"Yes, and I think she went to find him. Captain, there's something else…he may be the killer. She's got some serious research her and it all points to Thomas Grimshaw."

The Captain's eyes bulged and he quickly blurted out, "*Let's go people…on the move…now! We've got to find Bridges. She may be in danger. Move it, move it, move it!*"

On route to Garraty's house, the dispatcher radioed in and said she got a report of an intruder being killed.

"Have patrol take this one Bridgett, I have to find Bridges and we are on a sting right now—"

"I know Captain. I think it's your guy. Mrs. Deveraux called it in and she said she killed a guy named Tom," the dispatcher stated.

"Tom…Thomas Grimshaw?"

"She just said Tom, Sir," the dispatcher confirmed.

"Sgt. Willowbee. Sgt. Willowbee, are you there," the Captain switched channels and shouted through the radio for Sgt. Willowbee to respond.

"Go ahead Captain."

"You and Edwards continue to the suspect's house. I will radio for SWAT to meet you there and Det. Jarrod and I will go check out Mrs. Deveraux's place…*you got it.*"

"Yes, Captain," Sgt. Willowbee confirmed.

Mrs. Deveraux's mansion was dark and mysterious. The darkness was not gloomy or repulsive, it was seductive and intriguing. Even the exterior of her home manipulated your senses just as she would. You were completely captivated. You found yourself being drawn pass the black ten foot wrought iron gates and blown toward the enchanting French doors. But as Captain Crawford and Det. Jarrod entered the home, there was nothing enchanting about the horrific state of ambiance in the air.

Weapons drawn, spotlights blaring, Det. Jarrod and Captain Crawford slowly crept inside and called out to Mrs. Deveraux. There was no answer. Captain noted that it would be impossible for them to search this massive mansion alone so he quietly radioed for backup.

Moving a few steps further, they could see a body lying on the dining room floor, presumably male, Det. Jarrod thought. With several more steps, Det. Jarrod abruptly stopped in his tracks and indicated that he had heard something. It was Mrs. Deveraux, but he didn't know until they made it to the master suite and saw her lying on the floor, traces of blood all over the floor and a male body sitting upright next to the bed partially slumped over.

Captain Crawford ran to Mrs. Deveraux's badly injured body, "Mrs. Deveraux...Mrs. Deveraux can you hear me?" he said urgently.

"Yeah, Cap...tain."

"I called for help, is there anyone else in the house?"

She motioned her head, no.

"You hang on Mrs. Deveraux, help is on the way. You hang on dammit." Captain Crawford demanded.

EMTs worked on Mrs. Deveraux's injuries and at one point, they lost her. After reviving her, they rushed her out of the home and into an ambulance. On the way to the hospital, they lost her again.

"BRIDGES, I'M SO glad to see you," Det. Jarrod stated as he stood next to her hospital bed.

"I am glad to be here," she softly replied.

Det. Jarrod gave her a boyish middle school grin and looked her over from head to toe.

"Did you guys catch him? The killer?"

"Yes we did, thanks to you," Det. Jarrod confirmed.

"I don't follow…"

"Let's just say that you followed the paintings and I followed you." Det. Jarrod laughed and Bridges soon followed.

"Ouch…please, don't make me laugh."

"Sorry. But it feels good to hear you laugh. Doctor saids you gone be just fine Ms. Lady and I will be here with bells on to drive you home once you're released," Det. Jarrod insisted.

Bridges glanced over at Det. Jarrod, eyes hinted at a possible tear and whispered, "I would like that." An awkwardness came over them and Bridges cleared her throat and moved her eyes to her lap. After a couple of minutes had passed she asked, "What about Mrs. Deveraux?"

Det. Jarrod's face tightened and his expression of pity took over. Bridges looked over at him and her childish heartfelt sentiment inflamed her eyes and she found herself oddly frighten by what Det. Jarrod would say.

"She was very badly beaten."

She gasped and demanded he continue. "They lost her twice but the EMTs were able to revive her. She suffered broken bones in her face and she was almost reconfigured."

All Bridges heard was, *"They lost her…"* She had not listened to the other information that spilled from Det. Jarrod's mouth.

"Who was the killer?" Bridges slowly and softly whispered.

"It was Anthony Garraty. It seemed that the psychopath was stalking Mrs. Deveraux. Apparently, he suffered a brain injury as a child at the hands of an abusive family and he returned for his revenge. It is still uncertain, however, why he chose Mrs. Deveraux but we suspect it was because of her involvement with the Grimshaw Estate. It is also still unclear as to why he chose these victims and why he had to mutilate them. But forensics is combing through the evidence now."

"*Thomas.*" she said, struggling for another diminutive breath. She stared into the air for a while before Det. Jarrod's soothing voice brought her back.

"*Thomas*…Thomas Grimshaw?"

"So…Thomas is Garraty."

"Yes, we determined that, thanks to your research and we quickly scanned the information you left up on your computer screen. Oh…and you were right about those damn paintings. In his art studio, we found frozen blood from other donors, unfinished art pieces (that were very good I might add), and a final piece that was titled *Masterpiece*."

"Masterpiece…" Bridges gave Det. Jarrod a puzzling look.

"Yes, Masterpiece, and it was a series of words and a picture of a woman, whom we suspect must have been his mother. All the evidence was sent to the FBI lab for further analysis."

"The woman wasn't Mrs. Deveraux was it?" Bridges asked softly.

"You know, it did resemble Mrs. Deveraux, but no, we don't believe it was her."

"Mrs. Deveraux…" Bridges softly whispered while resting her head on the pillow.

"She should recover, but she will have to have corrective plastic surgery."

"*So, she's alive.*"

"Yes, that's what I said, but she's barely hanging on Bridges. Doctors are hopeful but she suffered a serious beating."

"What about Sgt. Willowbee?"

"What about him?"

Bridges gave Det. Jarrod a coarse look and said, "I saw Sgt. Willowbee…well…I believe Sgt. Willowbee was helping Mrs. Deveraux."

"You're right."

"I was…but what do you mean and why are you saying that like it was a good thing," she said keenly.

"He had to, orders from the Governor."

"The Governor, *why*," she said inquiringly, repositioning her body in the bed to sit up straighter.

"Mrs. Deveraux is highly protected Ms. Lady and Sgt. Willowbee was just following orders."

"Is this official?"

"Nothing is official, but is it ever when it comes to powerful people." Det. Jarrod smirked and interlocked his hand inside hers. "I wouldn't worry about it if I were you. Sgt. Willowbee is days before retirement and plans to put this all behind him and so should you." Bridge glanced up at Det. Jarrod with looks of sentiment and for the first time, she felt he actually cared for her. Her eyes gave him the sign of approval and Det. Jarrod produced a boyish grin. He nestled his hand deeper inside Bridges' hand and gripped her fingertips tighter.

"Hey young lady. If this is your way of getting off work you can forget it," Captain Crawford yelled as he walked through Bridges hospital room door.

"Hey Captain." Bridges said quickly while trying to cover her sudden moment of intimacy with Det. Jarrod. "I think I can be a little more creative than this." Bridges laughed while grabbing her shoulder.

"We got him. Which I'm sure you very well know by now," Captain said looking over at Det. Jarrod. "We finally got that damn nut job…well, Mrs. Deveraux killed his ass." The Captain chuckled and placed his hand on Bridges left forearm, "But you did it young lady. You found him and I'm sure Det. Popper would be pleased. All of us are pleased."

"Thank you Captain. It means a lot to me to hear you say that."

Masterpiece...

"The key to the Beauty and the hatred behind my Masterpiece is the intriguing, misunderstood, confused, disgusting, powerless, scandalous, but loving vivid, bold, and sometimes Lifeless essence that harbored the Beautiful enchanting Helen Grimshaw that is my **Mother!**"

—*Thomas Grimshaw*, May 1

Months Later

THE DOOR TO Senator Joy's private home office squeaked noisily as the perpetrator crept inside. The Senator looked up and a staggered reaction engulfed his face. His heart raced rapidly. His mouth struggled for moisture. He had reached an unprecedented level of fright that could not be ignored.

"I almost didn't recognize you. I thought you were dead," Senator Joy managed a spoken word through his dry mouth.

"And I thought you would never have the balls to double cross me, but I see I was wrong too," the perpetrator explained.

"In all the years that I have been in Office, I had never had to encounter anyone as methodically sophisticated as you. You have been something entirely different," the Senator said with a joyous jester.

"Humm…" the perpetrator smiled.

"What do I owe the pleasure of this visit?"

The perpetrator slowly walked over to the Senator, nestled against the Senator's desk, leaned forward and softly whispered a few last words near the Senator's ear, "I promised I would put a knife through your heart." Simultaneously, the perpetrator reached across the desk and with one violent thrust, shoved an ice pick through the Senator's chest.

CONGRESSMAN PHELPS' OFFICE sat just off the corner, next to the main courthouse in one of many Federal Buildings in downtown Birmingham. The perpetrator walked in as a concerned citizen and was directed to the fourth floor. No one knew how the perpetrator bypassed heavy security or the passerby's that swarmed the office building at twelve forty-five in the afternoon. The perpetrator slithered inside the Congressman's office, moved stealthily toward the Congressman's desk and startled him out of his skin.

"I didn't hear you walk in. My goodness, you startled me," Congressman Phelps said while trying to catch his short winded breath.

"Does my appearance surprise you? You seem a little on edge, even for someone in your position," the perpetrator indicated.

"I thought you didn't make it," Phelps said.

"I had to fulfill a promise," the perpetrator replied.

"And what might that be—"

Congressman Phelps' sentence was harshly disrupted by a swift stab to the chest. Phelps wheezed and wrapped his right hand over the ice pick handle and unsuccessfully tried to pull it out of his chest. In his final moments of life, the killer moved in closer to Phelps' ear and said, "I had to confront the ghost and put a knife in his heart."

a note from alina

efore I completed my first published novel, *Deceptive Men*, I was working on the outline for this book. It had only taken me a matter of days to develop the characters, the plot, and the story. I thought I had it in the bag. But as I restructured the outline of the book that you are now holding, I was hit with a burst of fresh air. It was amazing. I suddenly realized that I wanted to do more with this book. After a few months of letting the pages of my outline sit in a file on my hard drive; it finally came to me that I wanted Mrs. Deveraux to be more than just a rich woman with greed in her heart. I wanted her to be sophisticated, undeniably wanting, very beautiful, extremely powerful, manipulative, and certainly unforgettable. I wanted the story to take you on an eventful ride that you surely wouldn't want to end. I needed the story to be more than just another murder mystery—it had to be spellbinding and authentic with an incongruously seductive twist. And most of all, I thrived on it being entertaining and a darn good read. I hope that I have accomplished this as you read through the pages.

AS ALWAYS, I am most deeply grateful to my family who had to endure so much while I completed this novel. I also would like to send my thanks to the *Roy and Helen Hall McKinney Memorial Public Library* in McKinney, Texas for their unknowing generosity in helping me with my research for this book. Although the story takes place in Michigan, there were so many other elements that I had to research before this book would come to life. I found everything I needed and more in the *McKinney Memorial Public Library* system.

ALTHOUGH THE CHARACTERS in this work are fictional, **bleeding disorders** are very **real** and life threatening. There are several types of bleeding disorders but the most severe is *Severe Hemophilia Type A* which is a rare disorder in which the blood does not clot normally. *Hemophilia* can damage the organs, tissues, and muscles; especially when bleeds form in the knees, elbows, and ankles.[1] Other risks are loss of vision from bleeding in the eye, neurologic or psychiatric problems, and death that can occur from massive blood loss or bleeding in the brain, such as intracranial hemorrhaging.[2]

Most bleeding disorders, such as *hemophilia*, are inherited and is typically caused by an abnormality in the blood clotting factor or platelets which helps our blood clot when we suffer an injury. Some of the symptoms of a bleeding disorder are: excessive bleeding or easy bleeding, excessive bruising, nose bleeds, and abnormal or **heavy menstrual cycle**.[2]

On average, 1 in every 1,000 boys have *hemophilia* and about 75% worldwide receive little or no treatment due to the high cost of medication and insufficient care facilities that are not aware of hemophilia and the impact is causes. Medications for a child with a bleeding disorder such as *hemophilia* can range up to about $9,000 + per week when on a treatment therapy regiment. This does not include spontaneous bleeding episodes, which can occur at any time, especially with children who are diagnosed with *Severe Hemophilia Type A*, which is the most common. Even though *hemophilia* primarily occurs in boys, bleeding disorders affect men and women equally. A bleeding disorder can also be caused by: an immune system disease, liver disease, an antibiotic that is an immune system protein that can destroy blood clotting factors and blood cancers such as leukemia can all cause a bleeding disorder to form.

With the rarity of bleeding disorders, it is very challenging for the families that have children who suffer from a bleeding disorder. For more information please visit A'cardo Corp - www.acardocorp.org or the National Hemophilia Foundation located on the following page.

Although this is a product of my imagination, I would like to give credit to a number of **sources** that aided me in my writings:

[1]A'cardo Corporation. (2012). About bleeding disorders.
Retrieved from http://www.acardocorp.org/
bleedingdisorders.html

[2]National Hemophilia Foundation. (2012). What is a
bleeding disorder? Retrieved from
http://www.hemophilia.org/

Prose, Francine. (2005). Caravaggio: Painter of Miracles.
(1st ed.). New York, NY: *HarperCollins Publishers*.

SCALA Group S.p.A. (1991). The Library of Great
Masters: Caravaggio. (rev. ed.). Boston, MA:
Riverside Book Company, Inc.

www.ingramcontent.com/pod-product-compliance
Lightning Source LLC
Chambersburg PA
CBHW051423170626
46809CB00006B/2301